All names , charactors, places and events are products of the author's imagination and are not to be construed as real. Any resemblance to actual events or persons is entirely coincidental.

Scripture quotations are from the Holy Bible, New International Version®.

Second Chances

E.S. Holmes

CHAPTER ONE

The whirring and rhythmic beeping of the monitors could have put Ellen to sleep if it weren't for the fear gripping her heart. How had things come to this?

Ellen walked over to a table beneath the windowsill on the opposite side of the room and looked over the outpouring of love for this guy. Many flowers, cards and balloons graced the table, showing how he truly touched people's lives. The reality of how badly she had screwed up hit her, making her heart ache.

She grabbed a card off the table and opened it up. The inside was filled with signatures from a local third grade class. He was big on helping small communities and investing time in the lives of kids. "They are our future," he stated in many of his press conferences. The kids all wrote a sentence or two, saying how much they wanted him to get better and get back on the field again. Ellen could picture him now, standing up at the podium with passion filling his eyes, as he talked about the kids.

She set the card back on the table and grabbed another one. This one had a picture of a football lying in the middle of a field, no one in the stands or on the field. On the inside it said, "We need your presence back out there. It's not the same without you." The next card had a large bouquet of roses on the front and on the inside read, "We know you can pull through this. Prayers are being sent up! We love you."

The sun set outside as one by one Ellen read the cards saying how much Ryan was missed and how much he needed to get better soon. It had already been three days.

The monitors around him started to beep faster, turning into a sheer, solid beep after a few seconds. Panicking, she jumped off her chair and threw the card she had in her hands to the floor. Shouting for someone to help she went to his side and grabbed his hand, tears falling down her cheeks. "No, no you can't go yet! I haven't had a chance to say I'm sorry."

Two nurses came running into the room; the doctor close behind. They checked the machines and nodded to each other. What does that mean? Is he gone? She thought to herself. Fear gripped her and she felt like her heart might burst. One of the nurses came over to her and calmly stated that they needed to take him back to ICU and she was going to have to leave for the time being.

"No, I don't understand! I thought he was doing better!" Ellen squeezed his hand tighter. How could they be so calm about all this? Didn't they understand the pain she was feeling right now? The fear she was suffering from?

"Ma'am I'm sorry, but his neurological functions are failing and we need to take him to ICU to monitor him more closely and to give him the treatment he needs."

Ellen reluctantly let go of his hand as the nurses rushed him out of the room and out of her sight. She sat back down in the chair by the window and covered her face. The tears came in waves and she wasn't sure she was going to be able to stop them.

She wasn't sure how long she had been sitting there when she felt the faint touch of a comforting hand on her shoulder. She glanced up and locked into the soulful eyes of Ryan's mom. The tears started falling again.

"Mrs. Salas, I'm not sure I can get through this. I feel so helpless."

Mrs. Salas didn't say a word. Instead, she pulled a second chair next to Ellen and wrapped her arms around her, stroking her hair in consolation.

Ellen rested her head against her shoulder and let the sobs ravage her body. All she wanted was a second chance, a chance to reconcile with him, a chance to tell him how wrong she had been. Now she wasn't sure if she was going to get that chance and her heart was breaking into pieces because of it.

"Ryan, I'm sorry," she whispered.

A few minutes later, the doctor returned to the room to give them an update.

"It seems that Ryan has taken a turn for the worse. The swelling in his brain has put pressure on the brain stem causing a loss of brain activity. At this rate, we are not sure of the damage and we won't know anything until the swelling decreases. He is on medication to reduce the swelling, but the signs are not looking good. Even if he comes out of this, the amount of damage he has suffered will more than likely put him in a full vegetative state. I'm sorry." He turned and walked back out of the room without even a sympathetic glance back at them.

The tears came in torrents now as Ellen realized the horrible truth that was unfolding in front of her.

Ryan's mom and dad stayed in the room with her as the three of them tried to comprehend the news the doctor just shared with them.

"Mrs. Salas I don't understand."

"Sweetie, you know you can call me June," She pulled away and looked Ellen in the eyes. "Things in life don't always happen the way we think they should and this is one of those times. We need to pray for God's will in this situation. He is capable of miracles and I have to hope that Ryan still has a chance." Tears rolled down her cheeks as she spoke.

"I understand what you're saying, but I just don't think the God you're referring too would have allowed this to happen in the first place. After everything I have been through in my life, I just don't see how your God is as wonderful as you say He is." Ellen didn't mean to come across that snippy, but she couldn't help it. She got up off her chair and walked out into the hallway, leaving Ryan's parents behind.

"Rick, I wish she could see how truly loved she is. That her past does not define her. That she is forgiven."

Rick wrapped his wife up in his arms, "I know sweetheart. We will pray for a miracle for Ryan and that Ellen will see the light and know that no matter what, she is loved."

Ellen Kane, a famous sports reporter, was now questioning why life had turned out this way.

She walked down the hall to the vending machine and punched in the numbers for a snickers bar. She put in her dollar and grabbed the candy bar as it dropped to the bottom. Taking a seat in the waiting area, she bit into it and tried to figure out what to do. Her chance was over. The doctor said Ryan wasn't going to come out of this and if he did, he would probably be in a full vegetative state. What kind of life would that be? He was so vibrant, full of life.

4

Ellen couldn't imagine him in any other way. Those bright green eyes full of passion for his sport, for his fans, for life itself. This was not supposed to happen to the great Ryan Salas.

The tears assaulted her again as she covered her face, surprised that she had any left after everything that had happened the last few days. At this point, she should be shriveled up like a raisin, no ounce of water left in her to shed. She leaned back in her chair and closed her eyes, trying to reverse time and redo life before the chaos and complications began.

CHAPTER TWO

She glanced around her room one last time before heading out; the place she had spent the last eighteen years of her life. The memories washed over her as she processed the emotions going through her. Yes, she was excited to be going off to college, starting a new chapter in her life, but a part of her heart would always reside here, in their little cottage, in Folly Beach, South Carolina.

She slipped into her flip-flops and grabbed the keys off the coffee table to her little, red Honda Civic. She walked out the front door, locking it behind her. The fresh, salty air hit her nose, reminding her that this would always be her home. She took one more deep breath as she watched her parents secure the last of her belongings in her dad's pickup truck. The sting of tears gripped the corners of her eyes, but she wouldn't allow herself to cry. The University of South Carolina, where she would be studying sports journalism, was only two hours away. She would be able to come home and visit on the weekends if she truly got too homesick.

Her mom, Meredith, came over and gave her a hug, "Are you ready to go?" She kept her hands on Ellen's shoulders as she waited for a response.

"Yup, I'm ready to go." Ellen smiled up at her, trying not to let the fear show in her eyes, but she knew her mom was aware of what she was feeling. Moms knew those things, regardless of how hard you tried to suppress them.

Her mom rode along with her up to the university, while her dad, Colt, followed behind them. The drive was easy; all highway once you got out of their little town. With the windows wound down and the wind whipping her long, dark brown hair, Ellen knew that life was about to become exhilarating.

Gracing the university were beautiful, historical structures. The columns supporting the buildings gave them an elegance that was unmatched compared to other universities. One reason Ellen had chosen this school was the simple fact that the architecture gave her inspiration to keep life simple, unobstructed by the crazy chaos this world possesses.

Ellen stepped out of her car and headed up to the main building to get information on the dorm she would be residing in and her room number. She had one roommate that she had been communicating with online named Katie Miller. She seemed like a very sweet girl and Ellen was sure they would get along really well the next two semesters.

"I can help whoever is next," a woman shouted over the roaring noise of the freshman students gathered in the common area.

Ellen walked over and made sure she had her identification to present to the lady; a Ms. Thompson it said on her name badge.

Ms. Thompson took her driver's license and typed some things into her computer. "Okay, it looks like you'll be staying in Wyndam Hall, room 314. Here's a room key and here is the information you'll need to receive your school ID and papers for orientation tomorrow. Enjoy yourself!" She gave a quick smile and shouted for the next person in line.

Ellen grabbed up all of her papers quickly and walked back outside to where her parents were waiting to unload her stuff.

"So, where are you staying sweetie?" Her mom asked as she approached her.

"Wyndam Hall, room 314, the lady told me." Ellen double-checked the paper in her hand as she answered.

"I believe that's the beautiful, brick building we passed on our way in here," her dad piped in. The slightly graying hair at his temples glistened in the sun as he pointed in the direction of her dorm.

She hopped back into her car, as her parents got into the truck and followed her to the building. The paper the woman had handed her had directions to the dorm and it was relatively easy to find. Her dad was right; the building was gorgeous. The bricks were a deep red, with weathered markings. The front lawn had striking maple trees, whose leaves were reddening around the edges, preparing themselves for autumn. There were log benches lining the sidewalk up to the front door and Wyndam Hall was etched into the building's exterior. Ellen was glad she was staying in one of the older dorms on campus. The old charm excited her more than a new, modern dorm would have.

She pulled into the parking lot located next to the dorm and for the next hour she and her parents unloaded all of her belongings into her third floor room. Her roommate Katie hadn't arrived yet, which was nice, because it gave

Ellen the chance to pick the side of the room she wanted. She picked the side with the larger window; the room had two. They made her bed with her newly purchased linens and hung her posters on the wall. A poster of Miami's football logo got center stage on her wall. She had been a fan since she was a little girl, just like her dad. Every Sunday, during football season, they would sit on the living room couch together with corn chips and her mom's homemade salsa, watching Miami play. It was something Ellen cherished, a bonding between father and daughter that she hoped would continue for years. Her dream was to get into sports journalism and hopefully, one day, be writing articles about Miami's games.

Once she had things set up in her room she headed to the dining hall with her parents, which was open today for freshman and their families, while students moved in. They chatted about the upcoming semester over grilled chicken salads. All three of them were trying to hold on to what was left of the day, not wanting to part with each other yet. Ellen knew she would be ok. They were only going to be two hours away, but the thought of being apart from her parents after the eighteen years they had shared together was a little frightening.

There were some students going around greeting the freshman and their parents, welcoming them to the school. Ellen wasn't in the mood to talk to other students right now. She wanted to revel in the time with her parents, before they had to head back to Folly Beach.

That's when he came over. "Hi, my name is Ryan Salas. I'm on this years' freshman greeting committee." He stuck his hand out to Ellen, which she nervously shook and then he offered his hand to both her parents as well. "Hi Ryan, nice to meet you. I'm Colt and this is Meredith, my wife, we're Ellen's parents."

"I take it that you're Ellen then?" He smiled at her.

"Um, yes. I am." She wasn't sure what her problem was. She never acted this weird around guys before, but there was something about those deep, green eyes of his made her heart flutter. Something about this guy was going to impact her in some way or another. She felt it deep down in her soul.

"Well Ellen, I really hope you enjoy your time here at South Carolina. It's a wonderful school. I'm sure I'll see you around." He winked at her before making his way to the next table and Ellen felt herself blush instantly.

"He seemed very nice," her mother commented.

"Yes, he was." Ellen played with the salad still left on her plate.

Colt and Meredith glanced at each other and grinned. Just as Ellen had felt, they too felt that Ryan was going to make an impact on their daughter's life. There was just something about him.

An hour or so later the goodbyes were shared between them and a few tears were shed, knowing that things were changing between the three of them. Ellen promised to visit on weekends when she could and focus on her studies. As her parents pulled away and headed back home, Ellen felt alone. Yes, she'd make friends, but right now, in this moment, she wished she were heading back home with them. Back to her bedroom with the ocean crashing right outside the window.

She headed into her dorm building and up to her room. After opening the door and switching the light on, she noticed that Katie had moved her stuff in. She was probably at the freshman welcome party that was going on in one of the buildings on the other side of campus, but

Ellen was more content to just lie on her bed and be by herself right now. She wrapped her arms around her pillow and closed her eyes, imagining the ocean waves roaring right outside.

An hour or two later Ellen heard the door creak open and she sat up to look. Katie tiptoed in and latched the door shut.

"Oh, I'm so sorry Ellen. I didn't mean to wake you." Katie apologized as she sat on her bed and slipped her sneakers off.

"It's okay, I wasn't really sleeping anyway."

"Oh good, well that makes me feel better then. Also, I've been meaning to ask you if you'd prefer to be called something other than Ellen." Katie shook her blond hair loose from her ponytail.

"Well, most people call me Ellie, so you can call me that."

"That's pretty... Ellie... Yeah, I like that better."

They continued to chat about their lives and when they finally called it a night, so they wouldn't be exhausted for orientation in the morning, Ellen was convinced that Katie would be a very good friend from this point forward in life.

"Ellie, I forgot to tell you something," Katie whispered into the blackness.

"Yeah, what is it?"

"When I was at the freshman party tonight, a guy named Ryan Salas was looking for you. First off, did you know he's the school's starting quarterback and he's only a sophomore? And secondly, he's freakin' gorgeous." Katie let out a small sigh. "Do you know him or something?"

"No, I don't really know him. He introduced himself earlier today. I'm sure I'll run into him again at some point." Wow, starting quarterback. That's impressive, she thought to herself.

"Oh, I'm sure you will," Katie said.

Slumber overpowered them then until the sun rose the next morning.

~*~

Ryan relaxed on his bed with his feet pulled towards him, the playbook resting on his legs. The regular season was creeping up on him and he needed to be prepared. The school had hired a new offensive coordinator over the summer and even though they had been back to school and practicing the last three weeks, Ryan still had plenty to go over. Glancing over some new running plays coach had installed over the weekend; he made note of the defensive fronts he needed to be on the lookout for to know when each of these plays should be called. They were easy to comprehend on paper; it was putting them into action on the playing field that was more challenging. Ryan had a knack for the game though. As a sophomore starter he was already ahead in the football world. Depending on how well he could play and advance his team the next two seasons, he could potentially enter the NFL draft a year early.

Last season the senior starting quarterback, Drew Gross, went down with a mid-season ACL tear. A devastating injury for someone that was looking to be a first rounder in the draft. Ryan was called off the bench to finish that game, but nerves took control of him and South Carolina ended up being beat 36-10. Ryan was upset with himself; he knew he could play better than he had. He was determined in the following game to prove to his teammates that he could take Drew's place.

After that one bad game, Ryan improved and led South Carolina to a number two ranking in the SEC conference. They went on to compete in the Orange Bowl where they lost 24-21 to Alabama. The freshman was making headlines and had people talking about his future with the words, "Hall of Fame," locked in. Ryan didn't let that get to his head though, finishing off his freshman season he knew he had a long way to go before talk like that would even become legitimate. He knew how people could go overboard with exaggeration when a player had a few good games.

He continued to look over the playbook, trying to focus, but the new girl Ellen, which he had met in the dining hall, continued to invade his thoughts. She was beautiful that was for sure, but he wasn't the type of guy to chase after girls. Yes, he was the starting quarterback and many girls fawned over him, but he was focused on bettering his craft and completing his studies. There was something about her though that captivated him and he was pretty certain that he would be seeing more of her. She was going to be in his life for a long time; he could sense it.

Knowing he wasn't going to be able to keep his eyes open for much longer, he set the playbook on his desk and turned off the light. He pulled his comforter up over him, the rhythmic snoring of his roommate the background noise to his night. As he closed his eyes, the last thing he pictured was the stunning brunette, before his thoughts vanished and he drifted off to sleep.

CHAPTER THREE

Ellen sat under one of the maple trees located behind her dorm. It was in a secluded section, away from students going in and out of the building, giving her some tranquility from the chaos of college life. She leaned against the rough bark of the tree, breathing in the sweet air that whipped through the leaves, causing them to tremble slightly, almost as if they were whispering secrets among each other. Ellen liked to take this time to rejuvenate herself, settle her mind and soul. She had survived three weeks of college so far, enjoying most of the moments. Some of her classes were a little tough, but that was to be expected and she tended to enjoy academic challenges. It stretched her mind and if she wanted to go far in this world, she needed to be tested.

She had her journal in her hands, a few lines scribbled down. Writing was a release for her, a way to pour out any emotion imaginable. This was who she was, every feeling she had ever experienced, recorded within in her journals.

Tonight was the first home football game of the season and Ellen had an assignment in her journaling class to record stats from the game and write a small article about it. It wasn't going to be published in the school newspaper or anything exciting like that, but it was a step in the direction Ellen wanted to go and hopefully one day her articles would be published for others to read. She wanted to make it good; wanted her professor to see the potential she had... or at least the potential Ellen thought she had. Doubts crept in her head at that moment, telling her that she had no idea what she was doing, but she wasn't going to let them control her. She shook the nagging thoughts from her mind and got up from her grassy nook against the tree. The football game would be starting soon and she needed to get a good seat so she could observe the entire field and all that might happen during the game.

She gathered everything she needed for the game out of her room: pens, paper and her voice recorder for those moments where she could talk much faster than she could write. Slipping into her tennis shoes and grabbing a sweatshirt off the back of the door, she headed to the stadium.

"Hey girl!" Katie came running up, her blond ponytail swishing behind her. "Ready for the game? I've never been to one before!" She sounded as if she were in fast forward when she spoke.

Ellen giggled, "Well, I'm sure you'll really enjoy it if you can slow down a bit," she teased her friend.

They walked arm in arm into the stadium and found seats near the field. It was a perfect vantage point for Ellen to write her article and as Katie put it, a perfect spot for her to scope out the cute football players.

Katie grabbed hold of Ellen's arm and excitedly pointed in the direction of the players' tunnel. "There he is! Your soulmate!"

She was referring to Ryan Salas, but since that day in the

cafeteria, Ellen hadn't really spoken to him other than an occasional "hi" during a passing in the hallway or on the sidewalk. "Katie, you're insane. I barely know the guy and you know I'm not interested in a relationship. I really want to focus on my education." Ellen scribbled down some notes about the atmosphere in the stadium, while Katie rambled on about the fact that she needed to have fun and get out of the books every once in a while.

"Sometimes you need to let loose and have fun. You have your whole life to be boring and blah. Now is not the time." Katie playfully punched Ellen in the arm and winked at her. "Seriously, don't let an opportunity pass you by that you'll regret never exploring."

"It's not like I'm some kind of hermit with no life, but yes, I promise I'll try to embrace new opportunities. Okay?" Ellen smiled at her, trying to appease her friend and get her to switch the subject.

Katie seemed satisfied with her response and starting talking to some of the other girls sitting in their section.

Ellen had never been the outgoing type; she had been satisfied being by herself and having one or two close friends to share life with, but maybe Katie was right, now was the time to embrace new things.

The commentator announced the starting line-up as the players made their way onto the field. Ellen jotted their names down and made sure she had room to incorporate their stats. The game started off fast, South Carolina scored 21 points in the first half, holding their opponents to a lowly field goal. At halftime, Katie ran to the food stands and grabbed them each a soda and some fries to share.

"I hope you like ketchup, because I loaded these babies up!" Katie plopped down next to her and started digging into the fries. "How's the writing going?" she asked with her mouth full. Katie wasn't the most well-mannered or neatest of people, as evidenced by the eruption of clothes in their dorm room, but Ellen had learned quickly to tolerate it. The girl was her own person and neat was not in her vocabulary, but Ellen bonded well with her. She was someone Ellen really needed in her life.

Ellen showed her what she had jotted down and tried to explain things, but Katie wasn't the biggest sports fanatic, so she wasn't really getting all the concepts Ellen was throwing her way, nor did she really care to understand. She just enjoyed watching the guys on the field.

The second half wasn't near as exciting as the first half had been, but South Carolina pulled off a win. The final score, 28-10. They had won the week prior as well, in Pittsburgh, so they were undefeated so far.

Ellen glanced up from her notes, the feeling of being watched gripping her. Her cheeks reddened a shade deeper as she locked eyes with him. He waved at her and weaved his way between players towards the fence that separated her from the sideline.

"I was hoping I'd see you here," he dabbed at some sweat running into his eyes. "Did you enjoy the game?"

"Yes, I did. You played an excellent game. I have all your stats written down right here." She waved the notebook above her head and then realizing how dumb that must have looked she quickly brought it back down to her side.

"You write?" he gave her a quizzical look.

"Um, yes, I have a sports article assignment for one of my classes."

"Ah, so you're a sportswriter. That's even better," he paused, wiping more sweat from his brow. "Maybe we can get together and talk stats at some point?"

"Ryan let's go!" his coach yelled from bench.

"Well I gotta go; I'll see you around Ellen." He waved goodbye to her and jogged over to the rest of his teammates.

Ellen tried to process what had just unfolded here in front of her. Had he just asked her out?

~*~

The next day, underneath her private maple tree, she worked on her article for class. Going over all her notes from the game last night, she smiled; proud of herself for doing something she loved. She might not be recognized yet, but some day she would be.

She starting typing paragraphs of information onto her laptop, completely oblivious to the people around her. Most students hung out in the community lounges on campus or in the fitness center, but there was a small field adjacent to her dorm that a few students would gather to play soccer or toss a frisbee around. Ellen welcomed the activity going on around her, giving her a sense of belonging even though she wasn't part of the activity.

Deeply focused on her work, Ellen barely noticed the crunching of leaves underfoot of an approaching student. She didn't bother looking up right away, assuming they were making their way to the field or into the dorm.

"Hey, can I sit down?"

Ellen glanced up, shielding her eyes from the sun. Ryan stood in front of her, waiting for her response to his request. She felt her cheeks grow warm, "Sure."

She saved her work and closed her laptop, not ready to

let anyone look at what she had written so far.

Ryan sat down next to her, pulling his feet towards him and resting his arms on his knees. His green eyes sparkled in the sunlight and his sandy blond hair was perfectly put into place, other than one strand that had broken loose in the breeze. He had a boyish charm that put Ellen at ease.

"Working on the article about the game?" He pointed to her laptop.

"Yes, I'm just about finished. A few final touches and some editing left to do." Ellen absent-mindedly starting tracing circles on her laptop, not sure what to say next.

"I'd love to see what you have written, if you'd be willing to show me?" He scooted a little closer to her, hoping she'd open her laptop back up and show him.

"I don't usually like people reading my work until it's completely finished, but I guess for you I'll allow a sneak peek." She suddenly felt a rush of exhilaration about the fact that someone honestly wanted to see her work. Her parents had been the only people in her life that seemed genuinely interested in what she did.

Ellen opened her laptop back up, as Ryan patiently sat and waited for her to bring up her editorial. She read what she had so far as Ryan sat beside her, intently listening and holding on to every word. Ellen would occasionally glance over at him to see if he seemed intrigued Every time, he met her eyes and nodded, urging her to go on. When she finished, she closed her eyes and let out a slow breath, "So, what did you think?"

The sun was starting to set and it put a soft glow on his face as he started a slow applause. "Ellen, that was fantastic. It sounded like something I would read on ESPN or something. The way you described the atmosphere of the game was so realistic I thought I was right back on the field again." He turned to face her, "You have a true talent. I mean it."

Ellen's heart started to race. Her writing was that good? She never viewed her work along the lines of something a professional sportswriter would compose. "Thank you, it means a lot to me that you would think that highly of my work."

He touched the top of her hand and caught her gaze, "I mean it Ellen, it's really good."

Ellen slowly pulled her hand away, fully aware of the electricity she felt when his fingertips grazed hers. She didn't want to make it look like she didn't enjoy his touch, so she gathered up her notes and put them in her bag, making it look like she had needed her hand.

"I need to get going to finish up some other homework I have. Maybe someday soon you'll see my work in the school newspaper."

Ryan stood up and brushed the back of his jeans off, "I'm sure I'll be reading more of your work." He hesitated a bit and rubbed the back of his neck, "Um, I was wondering if you'd like to go to dinner or something sometime? I have practice until six tomorrow evening, so I could pick you up here around seven. I understand if you don't want to, but I really wanted to ask." He folded his hands behind him as he pushed a stone around with the tip of his shoe, waiting to see what she would say.

"I'd enjoy that, but I want you to know that I'm not looking for a dating relationship." Ellen saw the hint of rejection flash across his features, but it quickly vanished before she could apologize for her bluntness.

"Well, it's a good thing that I make an excellent friend then." He smiled at her and shoved his hands in his pockets. "Seven tomorrow?"

Ellen wasn't sure what else to say or why she was stupid enough to say she wasn't looking for a relationship. Sometimes she wished she could keep her mouth closed. "Yes, seven tomorrow." She turned and walked towards her dorm, giving him a wave as he turned around and walked away too.

Why had she said that? She wouldn't even be surprised if he didn't show up tomorrow. What guy would want to pursue a girl that flat out told him she didn't want him? She sighed as she walked into her room and sat her stuff down. Plopping down on her bed, she stared at the white ceiling, contemplating why her mouth was so big and why she couldn't let things just happen. Katie had told her to embrace new opportunities and here she was rejecting the starting quarterback that truly had an interest in her.

CHAPTER FOUR

The coffee cup warmed her hands as she sat in a chair adjacent to his bed, watching the slow rise and fall of his chest. The caramel aroma did little to calm her heart, but anything to drown out the sterile smell of this place was acceptable. His parents had gone home for the night, but she felt a pull to remain here beside him. She couldn't bring herself to leave, knowing her role in the mess that had brought her here to this moment.

He was breathing on his own, but the doctor said he was nowhere near being out of the woods yet. Ellen found herself staring at his face, willing his eyes to open, hoping that by some miracle he would just be okay again. The doctor had come in about forty minutes ago to check all his vitals, but the subtle shake of his head told Ellen that things weren't looking any better.

Ellen sighed, willing away the tears again; she had to hold herself together. She leaned back in her chair, closing her eyes to the dreary hospital atmosphere and let herself fall back into the past, the happy part of her past, where her heart felt lighter and mistakes were absent.

~*~

Just as he had said he would, Ryan appeared in front of her dorm at precisely seven the next evening. Ellen had put on her favorite top, a black and white chevron-patterned sweater that hung loosely around her shoulders. Perfect for the brisk, fall evening. Ryan was dressed in a maroon sweater with dark jeans, his hair neatly in place and a huge smile on his face.

"Well, you clean up nice," Ellen teased him. She walked down the steps towards him, giving him a quick hug when he reached out for her.

"You look great as well. I'm glad I could pull you away from your writing." He fell in step beside her as they made their way across the parking lot to his Jeep.

"Honestly, it wasn't that hard of a choice. You seemed a lot more interesting this evening than my computer screen. Besides, it's better to step away from my writing for a bit and regroup than to kill myself for hours over it."

"I'm glad you chose me tonight." He opened up the car door for her and helped her step inside. "I hope you like pizza, because I know a great little place about twenty minutes away from here," he told her, as he got in and started up the Jeep.

"As a matter of fact, pizza is my favorite." The playful banter between them came so easily. Ellen hadn't felt this at ease with a guy since her high school boyfriend, Jeremy, but she was not going to think back to that right now. It just brought pain to her heart and she was here with Ryan now, someone that genuinely seemed to care about her and was nothing like Jeremy.

The conversation between them flowed easily as they drove down the highway towards Gino's, a small pizza shop in a quaint little town off exit 15. It wasn't the fanciest looking place, but Ryan claimed it would be the best pizza she had ever eaten.

"So, how'd you stumble upon this place?" Ellen asked, as their server showed them to their table and provided them with menus.

"Sometimes, after a frustrating practice, or when I just need to clear my head, I go for a drive. One night I happened upon this place and thought, 'What the heck? I could go for some pizza.'"

"So, driving for you is like writing for me... a way to clear your head, a step away from this crazy world." Ellen took a sip of her water as she waiting for him to answer. Being here with him, in this little pizza shop, warmed her heart and she wouldn't trade this moment for anything. This was the type of friendship she had longed for, someone to confide in, laugh with and that understood her.

"Yes, exactly! I also like to take time to go to the shore and just sit, watching the ocean waves, contemplating how awesome God is. I mean He's the reason I am where I am today."

Ellen hesitated with her response. She had grown up going to church with her parents, but she walked away from it around the age of fifteen. How could you believe in a God that allowed bad things to happen on a daily basis, even when people say He is in complete control? A loving God that allowed so many unloving actions to take place in this world? Seemed bogus to Ellen and once she was old enough to decide on her own, she stayed away from church. Yes, her parents had been disappointed in her, but they understood her decision and her desire to figure things out on her own.

"That does sound relaxing." Ellen smiled at him, not mentioning his comment about God, trying her best to avoid broaching a topic that could put a strain on their evening.

She could tell Ryan sensed her hesitancy, but thankfully their pizza came and he seemed to be content letting that subject alone. Ellen breathed a sigh of relief and took a bite of her pizza. Ryan was right; this was the best pizza she had ever had hit her taste buds. The gooey cheese and perfectly spiced sauce blended well with the pepperoni and sausage toppings. She nodded her approval of the yumminess to Ryan, as he also took his first bite. "See, I told you… best pizza you'll ever have." Ryan winked at her and they continued with some lighter conversation and finishing off the rest of their pizza.

Ryan took the top off his Jeep before they left the restaurant, "You can admire the stars on the drive back to campus. There's nothing like it, especially when I take some of the backroads."

He was right; the drive back to campus was awe-inspiring. With her hair whipping softly in the wind she kept her gaze upward, admiring the expanse of the sky and the millions of stars that dotted the dark backdrop. Peaceful.

They didn't speak the entire drive back, both of them caught up in the complete silence of the night. As they say, silence is golden, and in this moment, it truly was.

Ryan pulled next to the curb of her dorm and came around to her side of the Jeep to open her door for her.

"You're quite the gentleman." Ellen took his hand as he helped her from the car.

"I was brought up watching my dad treat my mom this

way and I made up my mind that no matter what, with any woman in my life, I would always treat her with chivalry and respect. That's what's missing in the world nowadays and I want to bring it back."

Ellen turned to look at him before heading up to her dorm. "Ryan, I think that's sweet of you and I appreciate it. The world could use more of you in it." She gave him a quick, little wave before heading up the steps, but not before she saw the slight blush in his cheeks after her comment. She meant it; the world truly did need more Ryan Salas' in it.

Katie was in their room when Ellen opened the door. "So, how was date night with the hottest guy on campus? Did you ever think you'd be dating the starting quarterback?" Katie sat anxiously on the edge of her bed, waiting for a detailed story.

"Katie, we aren't dating. We just went out as friends and I plan to keep it that way. I'm not looking for a relationship." Ellen grabbed her pajamas off of her pillow and made her way to the bathroom to change.

"Girl, I think you're delirious, but you can keep thinking that all you want. I'm calling it right now, friendship will be out the window. You're going to fall in love with that guy and I will be standing by your side when you two say 'I Do.'"

Ellen rolled her eyes and chuckled as she closed the bathroom door and latched it. Katie had a crazy imagination. Ellen was standing firm with friendship only; they were not dating. She had been hurt badly in the past and didn't want to ever go through that heartache again. Friendship it was and friendship it would be. Ellen was determined.

CHAPTER FIVE

The sunlight emitted its rays through the window, sprawling across Ellen's desk as she tried to focus on completing her last final of the semester. The warmth of the sun was a tease, toying with her mind about the temperature outside. Winter break was almost upon them now and this first semester had been a whirlwind of new things and new people. Most of the time Ellen wondered how time had passed so quickly, but she relished in the moments that she could, soaking it all in. She placed her pencil down and glanced over the last few questions. Her philosophy class hadn't been her favorite, but there were a few things that she had enjoyed learning. She walked up to the front, her final in hand and presented it to Ms. Daniels. "I believe I'm finished, and I just wanted to thank you for your help this semester."

Ms. Daniels whispered a quick, "You're welcome," and continued making some notes in her computer.

Ellen hastily walked back to her dorm, anxious for her parent's arrival. Her philosophy class was located in a building not too far from her dorm, one of the few classes within a quick walking distance. When she arrived back at her room, she packed the few things that she had left lying around. The students were told they would probably have the same rooms, come next semester, but they still had to take everything home so the cleaning crew could be thorough. Katie was her roommate for next semester as well, which Ellen was thankful for. The two of them had become like sisters over the past few months and there were stressful moments that she had gone through when Ellen wasn't sure what she would have done without her.

"Hey girl, your parents just pulled in. Would you like me to help carry some of your things down to their truck?" Katie asked, as she appeared in the doorway.

"Thanks girl, I would appreciate it." Before Katie could grab anything, Ellen walked over and gave her a hug. "Thank you again for everything this semester. It wouldn't have been this great if you hadn't been here."

Katie held Ellen out at arm's length, "Girl, you've been a huge blessing to me too and I'm always up for dragging you out for some fun."

As soon as Ellen reached her parents, she gave each of them a huge hug, expressing how much she had missed them. Visiting on the weekends as often as she would have liked had been challenging over the semester, especially when she had been offered an opportunity to write in the school's sports section of the newspaper. This required her to attend every home football game and occasionally travel to the away games. Her parents understood and were more than excited over her progress toward her goal to one day write professionally.

Ellen was ready to go home for a few weeks, back to her small hometown, away from the hectic nature of college life. She would have to go to one more football game during her time off, because Ryan had led their school to another semifinal playoff game, just as he had last year. If they were to win that game, they would move on to the national championship game. Ellen wouldn't travel to that game if they did make it that far; one of the seniors in the journalism field would be covering that game solely. Ellen was just thankful for the chance to work the semifinal game, even if it was alongside Sabrina, the senior that she reported the games with.

Sabrina was helpful, giving Ellen pointers in writing her columns, what to avoid, what to include, but Sabrina had an edge to her that Ellen tried to avoid. Any stupid mistake that Ellen made could reflect back on Sabrina and Sabrina did not take that lightly. Also, the fact that Ellen and Ryan had become such good friends irked Sabrina. Ellen had overheard her talking to a fellow journalist, saying that she didn't understand how someone like Ryan would spend his time with a freshman, a nobody. Ellen tried not to let her feelings get hurt by that comment. Ryan was her friend because he wanted to be and she didn't allow herself to dwell on someone else's opinion. Sabrina was just jealous and Ellen let a smile cross over her face when she thought about that fact.

No, she and Ryan were not dating, even though Katie had other ideas with that. They had become really close friends over the semester, spending a lot of time with each other when they could.

The spring semester would allow them more time together with Ryan not having football to take up so much of his life. Ellen had kept herself busy with her schoolwork and articles, so with everything going on between the two of them, they didn't have a lot of time to focus on what they might be missing together.

Ellen reflected back on the semester as they made their

way back home; her parents were behind her, in the truck, loaded up with all her things. It took her back to the memories of driving up to the campus for the first time. So much had changed now.

~*~

The first week back home had been a blessing, time that Ellen needed to reconnect with her family and a few friends that she had left behind. Jackie, her next-door neighbor, had been over countless times bringing baked goods and new recipes she wanted Ellen to try. "I just want to make sure I have everything perfect for Christmas this year," she would say every time she stopped by.

Jackie was an older woman, in her late sixties, and she did her best to spoil the entire neighborhood with her treats. Every year, for as long as Ellen could remember, her parents and she would go over to Jackie's little cottage on Christmas day, with a few other neighbors to partake in a grand feast. Ellen looked forward to it every year and this year was no exception.

Today, one of the warmer days since her return, Ellen made her way to the beach, wearing her sweatshirt from college, just soaking in the salty air. She had missed this. Couples would stroll past her, and occasionally she would hear little kids screaming in delight over a sand crab scurrying along. She dug her toes into the sand a little farther, casting her face towards the sky, letting the sun bake whatever warmth it had left into her soul.

She had brought her notepad with her to get herself prepared for the football game coming up on Saturday.

She needed to make this last article of the season her very best. The man, Mr. Diggle, who ran the newspaper for the school, was very critical of her work. She understood that he needed to be. The work in the newspaper reflected on his teaching abilities, but sometimes he could be a bit harsh with her, more so than the other students. Katie said it was because she was the best and was held to a hire scrutiny, but Ellen just feared he had it out for her. She couldn't let her doubts and fears suffocate her. She knew this was what she wanted to do and she needed to work hard if she wanted to get anywhere with it.

She opened her notebook and started jotting down some ideas and wording she could use, preparing herself for the different things that could happen during a game. She included some football jargon she had heard on ESPN to use in the article and made sure she had the players' names jotted down so she could record stats quickly during the game. Most journalists did not write this way, but Ellen felt a lot more prepared for a game when she had ideas jotted down ahead of time; mainly descriptive words or phrases she could use throughout her article. It kept her from stressing out while trying to complete everything in the 24-hour period they were given to turn in their work.

She let her eyes drift off the page, focusing back on the ocean, watching the sun inch closer to the horizon. She closed her notebook and let the soft breeze blow her hair from her face. The salty air, mixed with a hint of rich musk, wafted over her, causing her to glance behind her. "Ryan! What are you doing here?" She dropped her notebook on her towel and ran over to him, giving him a quick hug.

"I wanted to surprise you. I know we won't be seeing each other much during the football game and stuff, so I thought we could get some time in now. Plus, my parents are along and wanted to meet your parents. And don't worry, your parents already knew about this." He winked at her and they both sat down on her towel.

"Well it's an awfully nice surprise. Thank you." Ellen brushed some sand from her hands and wrapped her arms around her legs. "So, where are your parents right now?"

Ryan stretched his legs out in front of him, "They're already at your parents' place getting acquainted. By the way, whatever you mom is making for dinner smells delicious. She said we don't have to be back until seven, so we still have some time."

Ellen felt a hint of nervousness wash over her as she thought about the fact that his parents were here meeting her parents. It felt like in-laws meeting each other after their kids were engaged or something. Ryan and she were just friends. It felt strange. She had met his parents once before at a school function for the football team and they were very nice people, but she wasn't sure why they wanted to meet her parents. "Why'd they want to meet them? Ellen asked.

"They just thought it would be nice since you and I are such good friends. They wanted to meet your family and get to know them. My parents are all about meeting new people, making new friends. Plus, it saved me some gas money not having to drive here myself." His sheepish grin crossed his face.

"Why do you seem upset about it?" he asked her.

"I'm not upset; I just think it's weird I guess. We're just friends and the pressure of people saying or thinking other things about us… it just gets to me."

"What other things?"

"You know… the jokes about us dating and things like that." Ellen let the sand fall between her toes, trying to cover up the feeling of how dumb this all sounded. She should have left it alone and been more thankful for the nice gesture. "I'm sorry, this is all so dumb. Just forget I said anything." Ellen let out a nervous laugh and started to gather her things.

Ryan gently grabbed her arm, turning her to face him. "Ellie," he paused and looked her in the eyes, gauging her true reaction to his next statement. "What would be so wrong with that? Dating?" And that's when he saw it... the pain that shot across her features and a darkness that shrouded her eyes.

CHAPTER SIX

Ellen had no desire to dive into her past, not now, not ever, if she had a choice. The pain still rooted itself in her soul and her heart was pained as the memories rushed over her. No, she couldn't open it all up again.

"Ellie, what is it?" Ryan probed her with his eyes, willing her to open up.

"I'm sorry Ryan, I can't. I just can't." Ellen's chocolate-colored eyes pooled with tears, but she would not allow them to fall. She didn't want him to see her cry. She didn't want him to know, because he would never understand. She took a deep breath and stood up. "We need to head back if we want to make it in time for dinner. My mom was never a fan of tardiness." Ellen managed a weak smile, but deep down all she wanted to do was weep. Weep for what had been lost.

Ryan reached for her hand, silently showing that he cared. The strength that exuded from the simple gesture reassured Ellen that all would be okay. They walked home in silence and Ellen could see Ryan holding back the pounding questions, the curiosity raging inside him.

They reached her parents' front porch, but before Ellen

could walk inside, Ryan turned her to face him. He grabbed her shoulders gently, rubbing his thumbs slowly along her collarbones, his eyes showed a gentle compassion Ellen had not seen before. "Please know that I will always be here for you, a listening ear, a confidant. Anything you need me to be, I can be for you."

"Thank you." Ellen took in another deep breath and turned to walk in, but before she turned the nob she glanced back at Ryan, "I just don't want to share right now. I need you to understand that it has nothing to do with you. I just don't want to open a wound that may never close back up again."

Ryan nodded in silence; an understanding flickered in his deep green eyes.

The evening filled itself with lots of stories between the families, mostly of the embarrassing genre. Ellen had learned that Ryan had been severely afraid of cats when he was younger, afraid that each one would turn into a vicious lion and attack him. "In my defense, I was told by my brother that's what they did. Who was I to test out his story at five years old? If it had been true I wouldn't be sitting here today living out this embarrassment." Ryan winked at Ellen across the table.

"Good thing South Carolina doesn't have a cat as its mascot," Ellen teased him. Laughter erupted from everyone at the table and more stories from both Ellen and Ryan's childhoods were shared amongst them.

"I have one more to share about Ellen before we call this a night," Ellen's dad announced.

"Dad, no! I don't think I can handle anymore!" Ellen pleaded with him.

"Don't worry sweetie, it's a good one." His cheesy grin broke down her defenses and she allowed him to go on.

"One afternoon as I was cleaning out the garage, little Miss Ellen here decided to hop in my car and listen to the radio. Harmless you would say, but Ellen got herself comfortable and accidently kicked the emergency brake, releasing it. As you know, our driveway is on a slight incline. Well, needless to say, I had never moved so fast in my life. Poor thing was scared to death, but luckily, the only injury that day was a smashed frog in the driveway. That poor frog never had a chance though, never saw his demise, but don't worry, Ellen made sure we had a proper burial for it." Everyone found themselves dabbing at their eyes from the laughter that followed. Ellen herself couldn't stop giggling at the memory of her parents dressed up in their finest attire, laying that poor frog to rest.

The evening had been just what Ellen needed to get her mind back to the present, the happiness of the moments that were shared around the dinner table that night. The goodbyes were exchanged between everyone and Ellen found herself glad that her parents were able to meet Ryan's parents. She had been hesitant at first, when she expressed her feelings to Ryan about it at the beach, but now she realized the good in having their families come together as friends.

Ryan gave her a hug before he hopped into his parent's car. "I'll see you Saturday at the game. It wouldn't be the same without my reporter there cheering me on."

"Well I'm just there to gather info to write my articles. How else would you move forward in your career without my amazing journalism skills making you look good?" Ellen teased.

"Ahhh yes, because my skills on the field aren't near as good as you make them sound on paper." Ryan grinned and opened the car door.

Ellen put her hand on the edge of the door, keeping him from closing it. "Ryan, you're seriously the best player on the field at every game. Sometimes I think my writing can't even begin to capture the greatness." Ellen smiled at him as she closed the car door. In the fading sunlight, she could see him smile back at her through the glass. She gave him a quick wave as they pulled out of the driveway and headed north toward their home.

As she turned to walk back inside she caught a glimpse of her dad whispering something in her mother's ear. "What are you guys sharing secrets about?" Ellen asked inquisitively.

Her parents chuckled and shook their heads. "Nothing," they responded in unison.

~*~

Ellen watched the clouds roll by as she, a few other journalists, and the team made their way by plane to AT&T stadium in Dallas. They would be going head to head against LSU, to try to advance to the championship game.

The sun streamed through the window, warming her skin and filling her with a renewed energy. She was ready for this game, ready to show her skills as a writer and ready to watch Ryan lead the team to a victory. Yes, LSU was tough this year, but Ryan had a fight in him, as did the rest of the South Carolina team.

The plane ride was silent and uneventful, most of the players meditating and getting themselves focused on what was coming next. They had the talent to win it. They just needed to dial in and rally together, proving they deserved to be playing in this game.

The plane touched down and everyone made their way off the plane and towards the luggage carousels to pick up their bags. Ellen had only seen glimpses of Ryan since the starting players stayed together in their own group. The one time that they had made eye contact though, Ellen nodded her encouragement, letting him know that she believed in him.

Her hotel room was nice; higher end than she had been expecting. She was sharing it with Sabrina who happened to be in a good mood. Ellen was thankful, because she didn't want to deal with any drama. A few of the other girls wanted to explore downtown Dallas, so Ellen headed out with all of them to enjoy the rest of the afternoon. They had meetings to attend this evening and lights were out at ten. They needed to be well rested and at the stadium by nine the next morning.

~*~

The sun stretched its rays through the curtain in her room the next morning, making its mark on a new day. There was a lot she needed to do to get ready for the game. She pulled the covers down and set her feet on the plush carpeting. She tiptoed her way over to Sabrina's bed and nudged her awake. They got ready in silence, both fighting the nervousness and anxiety of the tough game ahead. Ellen had faith in the team, but they were the underdogs and would certainly need to prove themselves.

They made their way down to the hotel lobby and

waited for the bus taking them to the stadium. Ellen made sure she had her notebook and pens, as she tried to catch her breath. This was a big moment for her, for her writing career. She walked towards the bus and chose a seat towards the back, taking in the scenery of Dallas as they made their way to the stadium.

The atmosphere within and around the stadium was electric; the crowds of people were clothed in their team's colors, some sporting war paint across their faces. Ellen couldn't help but smile, knowing she was experiencing something very special.

She and Sabrina made their way to the section reserved for them, watching the teams warm up and run through some quick drills. Ellen spent time jotting down some notes about what she was experiencing and absorbing the excitement radiating from the fans.

Ryan made quick eye contact with her before the team headed back to the locker room to prepare their game plan. He waved quickly and jogged with the rest of his teammates back into the tunnel.

"He really seems to like you," Sabrina commented.

"We're just friends," Ellen responded, hoping Sabrina wouldn't bring up anything else.

Sabrina nodded and started talking to some other students in their section. They were seated right near the team bench, so it gave Ellen a good vantage point for everything that was going on.

The next hour passed quickly as Ellen interacted with the other students and went to the snack area for a soda, hoping it might calm her nerves. She made her way back to her seat just as they were announcing the teams, who were running onto the field from their respective tunnels.

Ryan caught her eye right before kickoff ensued and she

mouthed the words "You got this," letting him know that she was in his corner. He smiled and slid his helmet on, gearing himself up.

South Carolina wound up winning the coin toss, choosing to defer and receive the kickoff after halftime. The energy sparked in the stadium, as the kicker made contact with the ball. The game was officially underway.

CHAPTER SEVEN

The game had been like something out of a movie, an experience that Ellen would never forget. At halftime, South Carolina was down 24-3, the outcome looking bleak for them. Ryan had been struggling all day. His offensive line was not protecting him well and it did not help that the running game had sputtered to a complete stop. Ellen hadn't seen Ryan play like this before. He was usually running the offense with complete confidence, but today he was overwhelmed and frustrated. Ellen felt herself thinking positive thoughts for him, trying to spark the team for the second half. Truthfully there wasn't much she could do, except continue cheering.

The team appeared from the tunnel, ready for the second half and Ellen grinned. Ryan had his smile back, his determination. When she looked him in the eye, she knew he was about to do something spectacular. And spectacular it was.

Ryan came out with a force LSU was not prepared for. He tossed three touchdown passes during their first three possessions of the half. South Carolina's defense held LSU to two field goals, so with three minutes left in the fourth quarter, South Carolina was down by six points and only needed a touchdown to win it.

Ryan slipped his helmet on and led the offense onto the field. This was it, this was their chance to get the monkey off their back and make it to that final game. Ryan's first pass fell incomplete, and on second down Luke Rowe, their running back, only managed a two-yard gain. Ellen's blood pressure was on the rise. They had to win this, they had worked too hard to come back and then lose.

Ryan completed his next pass to the tight end Zack Eifer for ten yards, giving them a new set of downs and continuing their chances. Ryan dropped back again and was nearly sacked, but he managed to escape and run forward for a gain of six yards, but wasn't able to get out of bounds. The time was ticking down and with no timeouts left, the clock reached the two-minute warning. The team walked over to the sideline going over their game plan. Ellen couldn't even focus on jotting down any notes; this was all too intense for her to concentrate!

The small break was over and the team was back on the field. Ryan completed his next three passes, leading the team to the twenty-five yard line. Twenty-five yards away from a win. They clocked the ball with fourteen seconds left. That gave them about two chances to get into the endzone.

Ryan dropped back, looking for an open receiver. He launched the ball in the air, but it was dropped. Harold Douglass, his intended receiver, couldn't hold on to the ball. Ellen let out a sigh; this was it, they had to score here to win the game.

Ryan dropped back again. He dodged to the left to avoid the rush and scrambled towards the sideline. Ellen held her breath, willing him to throw the ball. Ryan planted his feet and tossed the ball into the air. The stadium went silent, everyone holding their breath in anticipation.

Running towards the back of the endzone was Harold Douglass again, but this time he caught it! Touchdown South Carolina! Ellen screamed louder than she had ever screamed before.

They watched their kicker kick the extra point to make the final score 31-30. The South Carolina fans erupted with screaming and began jumping up and down, ecstatic that their team was advancing to the final game.

Ellen watched the team celebrate on the field. They lifted Ryan and Harold up in the air, celebrating their winning touchdown that had just propelled them into a championship game that had alluded them for so many years.

The rest of the evening was filled with laughter and celebration, while Ellen hung out with students and some of her journalism friends. The team had some meetings to attend and then had their own celebration planned afterward, so Ellen hadn't seen Ryan since the game.

Later that night Ellen got herself ready for bed. They had an early flight in the morning to head back home.

"Well, that was an exciting day!" Sabrina said, as they were both washing their faces.

"Yes, that was definitely a memorable experience." Ellen washed her hands off and pulled her hair into a bun on top of her head. "Enjoy the final game. I really wish I was able to go, but I understand Mr. Diggle wanting you to go solo with that."

"Ellen, you are really good at what you do and honestly, the reason I can get so agitated and moody is because I'm intimidated by you. I feel weird admitting that to you, but your work is good, I mean really good. South Carolina is going to get itself an excellent journalist after I graduate in the spring." Sabrina turned to her and smiled. It was a genuine smile and it made Ellen feel so much more at ease.

"Thank you Sabrina, you have no idea how much that means to me."

Sabrina leaned in for a hug, which caught Ellen off guard, but she returned the embrace. "Girl, I'm serious. You have an incredible talent and if I was making the choice, I would send you to the final game to report it."

Ellen smiled and thanked her again. It really made her feel good that someone like Sabrina felt her talent was that praiseworthy. Ellen had always been one that struggled with self-doubt, but knowing how others felt about her writing really gave her the confidence boost she needed.

She sat down on the edge of her bed and turned on the bedside lamp. She started to go over her notes from the game. She smiled to herself. Ryan really proved his abilities today and Ellen couldn't help but beam with pride.

There was a light knock on the door and Sabrina walked over to open it. There was only about ten minutes left until lights out, so they weren't sure who it was. Ellen heard some soft mumbling as Sabrina conversed with whomever it was on the other side of the door.

"Ellen, it's someone for you." Sabrina turned and gave her a cheesy grin.

Ellen slid off the bed and walked over to see who it was. "Ryan! I wasn't expecting to see you," Ellen exclaimed. Sabrina shut the door and retreated into their room, leaving Ellen and Ryan alone in the hallway.

Ellen became very aware of the fact that she was wearing her pajamas, her cheeks turning a rosy color the more she became conscious about it.

"I really like your pj's," he commented, which made Ellen's cheeks go from rosy to full-blown red.

"Uh, um, thanks?" she stuttered.

"I just wanted to come see you before things got crazy with us advancing to the final game and everything. We won't be able to see each other again until the spring semester starts and even then we'll be busy with schoolwork."

Ryan looked down and slid his sneaker across the carpet, in a nervous gesture. Ellen wasn't sure why though.

She reached out and put her hand on his shoulder. His vulnerability showed in his green eyes, which really stood out against the grey sweatshirt he was wearing. "Ryan, we'll always have time together. We managed to find time even with your crazy football schedule this past semester." Ellen willed him to smile.

Ryan took in a sharp breath and then released it, his body relaxing just a bit. "I guess all I'm trying to say is that I'm going to miss you and I wanted to see you." He came forward and wrapped her in a hug. Not their usual quick hug that they had always shared, this hug showed how much he cared. Ellen sunk in to his embrace. It had been a long time since she had had a hug like this and if she was honest with herself... it felt good. It was soothing, reassuring and it finally hit her that this guy truly cared for her and that brought a single tear to her eye. She didn't allow it to fall, but she knew it was there and she knew why.

He backed away then and slid his hands into his jean pockets. "I really needed that Ellie, thanks."

Ellen folded her arms across her chest, trying her best to cover her pajamas up that she was still feeling self-conscious about. "I needed it too, Ryan."

45

She heard one of the teachers coming down the hall, telling students, "lights out," so Ellen turned to open the door. "Gotta go. I'll be cheering you on in the championship game. You're going to be great. I can feel it."

"The reason I won today Ellie, was because of you. Knowing that you're cheering me on will be what drives me in the next game. Just like today and every day."

CHAPTER EIGHT

January 1st. It was championship game day and Ellen was cuddled up on the couch with her dad watching the pregame show. This father-daughter time was something she cherished; a nostalgic moment, taking her back to childhood Sundays, watching Miami play. She enjoyed this time with him, listening to his comments about the reporters' opinions. Her dad rattled off some stats about Ryan that he had been keeping track of throughout the season. He had never been one to follow college football closely, but ever since she and Ryan had become such good friends, he had a new sense of wonder with the sport. Ellen hung on to every word, taking in his facial expressions, greying temples and the wrinkles at the corners of his eyes when he would intently stare at the television screen.

Her mom called them from the kitchen, interrupting them for a second, asking them what type of cookies she should make. Ellen and her dad responded in unison with their favorite, chocolate chip.

Kickoff was in about ten minutes and the aroma from the kitchen was making Ellen's mouth water. Her mom was an excellent baker, unfortunately a trait that Ellen had not received. Ellen couldn't even manage not to burn those pre-made cookies in the freezer section of the grocery store. Her mom made her way into the living room; her glossy brown curls were pulled back into a clip. She set a plate of cookies down on the coffee table next to the chips and salsa that Ellen and her dad had already dug into. It was their traditional football feast. Salty and sweet.

Her mom had never been the type to get into a football game. She usually would just pop her head into the living room and ask how Miami was playing, then would continue with whatever she was working on. This game was special though, because a young man that they all admired was leading his team in a championship game.

When a reporter interviewing Ryan appeared on the screen, Ellen felt her heart speed up. She figured it was from the excitement of the game, but deep down she felt it was something more. She couldn't shake the grin off of her face the whole time he was being interviewed. He expertly answered the interviewer's questions and never once made the game about himself, but unified himself with the team as one, solid unit. The moment he glanced directly into the camera before heading back to the team bench, Ellen knew he was looking straight at her. He told her she was his motivation and that was his cue for her to start sending strength his way.

As Ellen's eyes remained glued to the screen, her parents gave each other 'that' look. They knew the thing Ellen was trying so hard to hide. Her heart's walls were breaking down and even though it scared her to death, the exhilaration of allowing someone in her life again was overpowering her common senses.

The next three hours were spent doing a lot of cheering
and an occasional yelling spat at a supposedly blind
referee. The intensity of the game never died down. It was
neck and neck from kickoff to the final seconds of the
fourth quarter. But after all the ups and downs, South
Carolina had secured a championship victory, something
that had alluded the school for two decades. They had
won!

Ellen was beaming from ear to ear, because without
Ryan leading the way they never would have won. He had
been on fire since he first stepped foot onto the field in their
opening drive. South Carolina's defense had struggled the
majority of the game, but Ryan kept them in the game with
such finesse that Ellen wasn't sure she was watching the
same guy anymore. The precision he had with each pass he
threw, and the elusiveness he displayed while avoiding the
pass rush was something everyone had their eyes fixated
on. This kid was special and the millions of viewers
watching knew it.

When Ryan tossed the game-winning touchdown, Ellen
and her parents jumped off the couch and danced around
in celebration; elated at what they had just witnessed. Even
though Ellen would have loved to be at the game, this time
with her parents was more important to her. They gathered
together in a group hug and continued celebrating the rest
of the evening.

Later that night, Ellen could not sleep as she rehashed
the game repeatedly in her mind. She had always loved
football, but after today she had a new love for it and Ryan
was the main reason for that. She pulled the covers off of

her and tiptoed across her childhood bedroom, raising the blind on the window on the far wall. The sky was cloudless and the stars shone brightly on their inky backdrop. Ellen slid the window up to let the ocean air in. She took in a deep breath of its saltiness and let the breeze tickle the ends of her hair. The calmness wrapped its arms around Ellen, giving her a soothing embrace and willing her to let the walls around her heart tumble down. She knew the feelings that were surfacing within her and it scared her to death. Being vulnerable like that again seemed stupid and careless, like she hadn't learned the first time. This time was different though, Ryan was different. He cared for her, would do anything for her. He had voiced it to her many times. He was considerate of her feelings and never pressured her into something she didn't want to do or say. "He's not Jeremy," Ellen softly whispered into the breeze.

Ellen sat there staring up into the stars when her phone chimed. She walked over to her nightstand to glance at the screen. It was a text from Ryan asking if she was awake.

"Yes, I am." She quickly typed back.

A few seconds later, her phone lit up with a picture of his face, signaling a call from him was coming in. She answered quickly with a whispered hello, trying not to wake her parents.

"I just wanted to hear your voice." The sweetness of his tone carried through the phone to her listening ear.

"I've wanted to hear yours too." Ellen went on to congratulate him on his win and for the next hour and a half, they discussed the game and their plans for the next two weeks preparing to go back to school. Ellen let out a slow yawn, her body telling her that it finally couldn't elude sleep one moment more.

"I can hear you yawning through the phone. You must

be pretty bored with me," he teased. "Seriously though you should get some sleep, Ellie."

"You could never bore me Ryan." Ellen loved the way he said her name. 'Ellie' rolled of his tongue so beautifully.

"I'm glad I don't bore you. Who else do I have to speak to in this world that wouldn't make endless fun of me and my fear of cats?"

Ellen let out a burst of laughter and she tried to quiet herself quickly before she disturbed her parents across the hallway.

They talked for a few minutes more, neither one wanting to end their conversation. Ellen refrained from expressing what she had been experiencing earlier, not wanting to have a conversation like that over the phone. She wasn't even sure if she completely understood the feelings anyway and didn't want to blurt anything out that she could never recover from. She needed some time to ponder everything. Her head screamed to keep the solid friendship going, the logical thing to do, but her heart was screaming a completely different answer and the two were dizzying her with confusion.

They exchanged goodnights and Ryan promised to keep in contact as best he could with everything he had going on in the next few days.

Ellen shut her window and padded across the wood floor, back to her bed. She pulled the covers up to her chin and let sleep overtake her.

CHAPTER NINE

The holidays had passed much too quickly for Ellen's taste, as she set foot on campus again, mentally preparing herself for the coming spring semester. The break had been a wonderful time spent with family and friends, a mind clearing of sorts to declutter her brain from the previous semester. Here she was again though; ready to conquer this next semester. Her parents had just left after helping her lug all her belongings up to her dorm room that she was sharing again with her dear friend Katie. Katie lived in Colorado, a far off land compared to sunny South Carolina, so over the holiday break they had only kept in contact via a text message or phone call here or there. Ellen was eager to hug her friend and catch up on life.

She finished making her bed and organizing her clothing in the wardrobe along the far wall of their shared room. Luckily, Ellen didn't have a need for many clothes, just your basic staples to stay in the latest fashion trend. It left Katie with plenty of room to store her overabundance of clothes. Katie would be arriving later in the evening, so Ellen decided to walk down to the student cafeteria and grab some dinner.

The air was brisk as she made her way across campus. She pulled her jacket tighter around her, trying to block the breeze. The sun was lowering itself towards the horizon creating beautiful orange hues across the sky. The clouds positioned themselves strategically as if an artist had paused time and taken their brush, stroking the sky gently to create some contrast. Ellen paused to admire the handiwork. It was at times like this that Ryan would often comment on God's masterpieces and how His greatness was shown, even in a sunset. Ellen loved that he took his faith so seriously, it was one of the things she admired about him. No, religion was not something Ellen liked to talk about or even think about, but Ryan understood that and didn't pressure her, which she was thankful for. As she had stated to him many times over the last few months of their developing friendship, she didn't feel that faith in a God that could allow so many awful things would be beneficial to her and her life. It was good for him she guessed, but she could never accept something like that after all the things she had endured in life.

The cafeteria appeared in front of her and she hurried her last few steps to escape the bitter wind. South Carolina didn't have much of a winter in terms of snow, but there was always the chance of some nasty cold fronts dipping down into the area. The cafeteria was packed with students eating their dinner or just gathered around chatting with each other, catching up after the winter break. Ellen grabbed a chicken caesar salad off the salad bar, with extra dressing and a fresh roll, hot from the oven. Her mouth watered at the thought of devouring her food, realizing how hungry she truly was.

She nodded and said hello to a few students as she made her way to a quiet table in the far corner. The salad hit the spot and she sat there going back and forth in a debate with herself deciding on whether or not to get some dessert. She decided on a fudge brownie and after finishing that off, she decided to head back to her dorm room and wait for Katie to arrive.

As she briskly walked to her dorm, anxious to get out of the cold air, her thoughts turned to Ryan. She missed him for sure; she had no trouble denying that fact. They hadn't talked much after their phone conversation after his big win. She understood he was busy, but she wished his life would just slow down a little bit so they could squeeze in some time together. She knew she would run into him soon, she just wasn't sure when that time would come. Classes were starting in two days and Ellen was really hoping they would get some time together before then. She made her way up the stairs to her dorm room and flicked on the light after opening the door. Katie wasn't here yet, but she should be soon. Ellen sat on her bed and waited for her friend's arrival.

A few minutes later a bubbly Katie waltzed in the door and wrapped Ellen up in a giant hug. "Girl, I have missed you something fierce!" She immediately started talking about her adventures over her break, barely taking a break to breathe. This was what Ellen loved about her friend. She was her own person, full of energy and she somehow brought fun with her wherever she happened to be.

Ellen sat on the edge of her bed, listening to her friend's every word. Katie was going on about a ski trip she had taken with her brother and a few of his friends. "Andrew was super cute, but you know me... I don't want to settle down with someone yet. I want to spread my wings, live and love freely, enjoy my single life." Katie laughed as she popped open an orange soda she had grabbed from the mini fridge in their room.

"Oh, I'm sorry. Did you want something?" Katie asked.

"Sure, toss me a root beer."

Katie opened up the fridge again, grabbed Ellen a root beer and tossed it her way. She then continued on with her story about Andrew and the rest of her winter break adventures.

"So, enough about me. I know you and Ryan had talked a little over break and saw each other once or twice. Any more news in the realm of this budding relationship?" Katie pulled a pillow up to her chest, plopping her chin against the top of it, willing Ellen to spill some juicy news.

Ellen hesitated with what to say. She didn't want to say anything about her growing feelings, because she wasn't even sure she understood what was going on in the first place. She didn't want Katie to get any crazy ideas either. She decided to keep quiet about that for now, even though a small part of her was dying to tell someone.

Katie leaned forward, "Well? Anything?"

"No, nothing new at this point. We have a good friendship and I really enjoy the time I spend with him. He is someone that I really need in my life." Ellen stretched out on her bed. "As a friend, not something more!" She quickly added, before Katie could throw in her two cents.

Katie rolled her eyes, "If you say so." She chugged down the last of her soda and tossed it into the trashcan at the end of her bed. "I really think you need to let loose and just accept the fact that the guy likes you Ellen. I mean, really likes you. If you keep him in the friend zone, he may just walk away. No guy likes to get rejected like that."

"Ryan's not like that," Ellen explained. "He's a good friend and he always will be. I know it."

"Well okay then, maybe he won't leave you, but you

really shouldn't deny yourself an opportunity to date a really great guy."

Katie made a good point, but Ellen just couldn't let her heart go that easily. The fear of having it shattered again was too painful to even begin to think about.

"I may enjoy the single life and heck I know I make it look fabulous," she twirled her hand in the air to emphasize her point, "but Ellie, you're the type of girl that needs the security and consistency of a relationship. I can sense it in you. Smack me if I'm wrong, but I'm pretty sure I'm not." Katie traipsed into the bathroom, satisfied she had gotten her point across.

Ellen leaned back against the wall, taking in what Katie had said. She made sense in her crazy Katie way, and Ellen really needed to take a step back and think about all of it. Her past was a barricade between her and her heart's desire and she wasn't sure how to knock that wall down. It made her nauseous just thinking about bringing all that up again. She knew she would have to; Ryan deserved to know if she was going to move forward, take a chance. Ellen heard the shower turn on and knew Katie would be in there for at least half an hour. It would give her some time to herself, to think about what step to take next. She knew this for sure; she was falling for Ryan and she was falling hard. There was no doubt about it now, and that realization scared her to death.

She grabbed her cell phone and brought Ryan's contact information up. She hit the text box and typed out a message. *I'm ready to talk now, to share my story with you.* She hit send and that was it; she couldn't take it back now. She set her phone back down on her desk and leaned back into her pillow. She closed her eyes and thought about how she was going to do this. Spilling out her past to Ryan was going to be hard. Reliving that time of her life was going to be heart wrenchingly painful. The more she thought about it the more her eyes burned with tears. The images flashed in her mind, reminding her of that awful night.

Her phone buzzed, snapping her from the nightmare. She leaned over and snatched it off of the desk. It was Ryan's response, *I'm here for you when you're ready. Let me know when and where and I'll be there.*

She had to do it now before she backed out. There was no reason for her to keep this back any longer. It was time. *Tonight. Our field. At nine.*

She stared at the screen as she watched the message turn from sending to sent. In a few seconds his response came through, *I'll be there.* Those three words brought a comfort to Ellen that rushed a warmth over her body. They renewed her strength and gave her a sense of hope she hadn't had in a long time.

CHAPTER TEN

Their field was down a backroad, a place they had
discovered one evening after eating pizza at Gino's. The
wind had died down, taking the chill out of the air. Ellen
was thankful for the break in the cold as she stepped out of
her little Civic and hopped up onto the trunk, waiting for
Ryan's arrival. She leaned back against the rear window
and watched the clouds as they passed over the stars. It
had turned into a beautiful night. Unfortunately, this
evening would be marred by the nightmare of a memory,
but it was time for her to share. There was no need to keep
it to herself any longer and Ryan was the one person she
knew she could trust with anything, even her fragile heart.

She heard gravel churning under the approaching tires
of his Jeep, as he dimmed his headlights and pulled in next
to her. He opened his door, slid out with a blanket and a
thermos in his hand and made his way over to her. She saw
the hint of a smile on his face in the soft moonlight and it
warmed her heart.

"I brought some hot chocolate along to keep us warm, in
case the wind picks up again." He held the thermos in the
air indicating his thoughtfulness as he climbed up onto the

trunk with her and leaned back.

The expanse of the field in front of them met the inky horizon with a gentle kiss providing a peaceful surrounding, which gave Ellen the nerve to pour out her heart. They sat in silence for a few moments, as Ellen tried to calm her racing heart, not from nerves, but from the emotions welling up inside of her trying to break her down. Ryan placed his hand on hers, a gesture ensuring her that he was there to support her. "Whenever you're ready," he gently whispered.

Ellen took a deep, steadying breath and launched into her story.

~*~

She and Jeremy were celebrating two years together that day and Eric, their mutual best friend and forever third wheel, was in the process of snapping a few photos to commemorate the special day. His photography skills weren't exactly professional, but the fact that they were free was a plus and his work was decent enough to be able to frame and forever highlight the day. Ellen giggled as Eric had them pose against a tree, which released a shower of water when they bumped against it from the morning rainstorm. The clouds were still looming in the sky as the snapshots were taken, but so far the weather had cooperated with them and Eric was confident the pictures were going to look great.

Eric brushed his wild, blond curls from his eyes. "Jeremy, get the coat hanger out of your mouth and give me a natural smile." Eric snapped a few more, as Ellen playfully tickled Jeremy's ribs, enticing a genuine smile out of him.

"Dude, this is my natural smile," Jeremy retorted, as he dodged Ellen's jabs.

"Well sir, I've seen much better." Eric stood up after kneeling in the grass and tried brushing the mud stains from his jeans. "Good thing these are my ratty, worn out pair or grandma would kill me."

They moved over to an old, wooden picnic table that was located in the middle of the park where they were shooting and took a few shots of the three of them together. Eric had a tripod for his camera and could set his timer to get pictures of the three friends collectively, so they would have a few candid memories.

The three friends had been inseparable since the fourth grade and even though Jeremy and Ellen had begun a romantic relationship, the bond between them all was stronger than ever.

They spent the rest of the afternoon goofing off together, and watched the sun as it slid down to the horizon and then disappeared amongst the oranges and reds of the beautiful sky. The three of them lay there, talking about the future. Jeremy planned on going to the University of South Carolina to study sports broadcasting, while Eric wanted to attend the same school, but as an English major, using the degree to teach high school students in the future. It was only April of their junior year, so they had time before all of their plans would actually happen. As long as they were all together, they would be happy wherever life led them.

"You wanna go get ice cream down at Mario's?" Eric suggested.

"Sounds good to me." Ellen stood up from the ground,

brushing the grass from her jeans, noting that the dampness had soaked through. "I guess we should've brought a blanket." The three of them laughed and walked to the parking lot towards their cars. Eric had met them there earlier that day, so he got into his small, blue sedan, while Jeremy and Ellen got into Jeremy's red Mustang. Jeremy's parents were well off financially and had surprised him with the sports car for his 17th birthday. Ellen had thought it was a bit extravagant for a seventeen year old, but she wasn't going to complain, especially since she got to ride around in it all the time.

"Race ya there?" Eric taunted Jeremy through their open windows.

"Dude, you have no chance." Jeremy revved his engine to emphasize his point.

"We'll see about that." Eric slammed his car into reverse and peeled out of the parking lot.

Jeremy quickly responded as he too sped out of the parking lot. Ellen grabbed on to the door handle to steady herself. The adrenaline warmed her body as they prepared to race.

It was a wooded backroad to Mario's, so the chances of being pulled over were very slim, plus this wasn't the first time the three of them had had a competition like this. Jeremy caught up to Eric and pulled onto the left side of the two-lane road as he cruised by. Ellen waved at Eric as they passed him while they sped forward. Jeremy eased on the gas a little bit to go around a small bend in the road, but as he slowed, Eric took the opportunity to make the inside pass and regain the lead.

"On no he doesn't." Jeremy straightened the car out after the turn and sped up again, passing Eric for the second time. Mario's was about two minutes up the road, so he needed to maintain the lead to keep his pride.

A sharper turn approached them as they moved closer to the shopping center that housed their favorite ice cream shop. As Jeremy slowed to make the turn he heard Eric's engine groan in anger as he sped to regain the lead in the final stretch.

"What is he doing? He can't make this turn..." And that's when it happened. The loud screeching of straining brakes, the awful crunch of car metal as Eric's sedan struck a tree on the other side of the road and the horrific screams as Ellen watched what was happening unfold before her eyes.

"ERIC!" Jeremy slammed on his brakes, threw the mustang into park and flung his door open as his feet hit the pavement, running towards the crash. "Ellie, call 911!" He screamed as he ran faster towards the scene. Ellen reached for her phone, her shaking fingers barely made contact with the keypad. "Hello? Hello? Please, please come help my friend! There's been an accident!" Ellen screamed into the phone as the poor woman on the other end tried to calm her, asking for their address. Ellen was so panicked she couldn't think straight and her mind went blank. Her eyes couldn't look away from the horror before her. Smoke was billowing from the smashed hood of Eric's car and Jeremy was shouting for Eric as he tried to get the driver's side door open. The woman's begging voice seemed so far away, as tears blurred Ellen's vision and her body began to shut down. The phone dropped from her grasp as her body went completely numb. People from the shopping center down the street came running towards the scene. Three burly men pulled Jeremy away from Eric's car, begging him to wait for the ambulance. The sirens wailed in the background. Ellen wasn't even sure how they knew where they were considering she had never answered the woman's questions. Probably GPS tracking she thought, as she sat in her seat, frantic and helpless.

Everything unfolded in slow motion, or so it seemed for Ellen and Jeremy. Jeremy held her close as the two of them leaned against his car watching the authorities and EMT's do their job. They had ripped Eric's door open and retrieved his body from the vehicle. Ellen gasped and a new flow of tears started as she saw the blood caked onto Eric's lifeless body.

"He's still breathing," one of the EMT's shouted, as three more rushed over with a stretcher and loaded him into the ambulance. It sped away with the harsh sound of shrieking sirens. Slowly the police officers began to approach them to ask questions. Ellen couldn't even concentrate enough to answer their questions, but Jeremy calmly explained the details of what had happened, trying his best to maintain control of his own emotions. He conveniently let out the fact that they had been racing, which Ellen didn't understand, but she figured the police knew that anyway and didn't bother saying anything about it. Besides, she was so emotionally drained she couldn't form a complete sentence to begin with. All she could think about was her friend's bloody form being lifted from his car.

Three days later Eric died in the hospital with Jeremy and Ellen right by his side. The sobs tormented her body as the solid beep indicated his passing. She couldn't shake the guilt that took over her body in powerful waves. She had killed her best friend. He was lying here dead because she didn't do something to stop it. An ear-piercing scream escaped her lips as her heart shattered. She pounded the bed in anger, screaming for Eric to wake up, for his blue eyes to shine, for his hearty laugh to fill the room again. She wanted her best friend back. "This isn't happening," she whispered between sobs. The doctor and nurses ran into the room at the sound of her screams. They rushed to turn off the machines, checked his pulse, and did whatever else they do in a moment like this. Ellen didn't seem to care about anything other than the subtle nod they gave each other signaling the demise of another patient.

She yelled at them "That's my best friend! Can't you do anything?" Jeremy wrapped her up and tried to calm her. She didn't have the energy to fight him and collapsed in his arms from the weight of her heavy heart.

Eric was gone.

CHAPTER ELEVEN

The sky itself cried that day; the weather a mirror image to Ellen's soul, as Eric was laid to rest. She stared intently at the wooden coffin, lilies and roses graced the top, as the pastor went on and on. Ellen barely heard a word of the pastor's monotone message. All she wanted was for Eric to jump out of the casket, disproving his death to all of them. The pastor, Allen she believed was his name, was going on about God's plan for each of us. How even though we, as humans, deem this as taking a life too soon, it ultimately is a part of God's elaborate plan. Ellen rolled her eyes beneath her hooded jacket, feeling anger towards the pastor's emotionless speech. He didn't know what he was talking about, if this so-called God thought a premature death was a grand idea then Ellen wanted nothing to do with Him. Her parents always tried to get her to go to church with them, to share in their faith again, like she had as a little girl, but Ellen wanted nothing to do with it. That's fine and dandy if it makes them happy, but Ellen couldn't forgive someone that took her best friend away from her.

Pastor Allen finished speaking and everyone made one

last walk by the casket. Jeremy held Ellen's hand, as they were the last two to approach Eric's final resting place. Ellen glided her hand over the glossy finish and whispered a few, loving words to her friend, "Eric, you'll always have a special place in my heart. No one with be able to replace your presence in my life. I'm going to miss you." She sniffed as she finished that last sentence and her vision blurred as the tears began to flow freely again. She thought she would have been done crying by now, but nothing was going to ease the grief in her heart.

Jeremy walked over to his mustang, but Ellen stayed back a few moments and walked over to where Eric's grandmother was standing. Eric's parents had died when he was young, so Nora had been his only family.

Ellen approached Nora and wrapped her in a warm embrace. She felt frailer than before, but she knew that Eric's death was taking a toll on the poor woman. She had already lost so much in this life and to lose the only family she had left was heartbreaking.

"Nora, I'm so sorry. I wish there was something I could do to bring Eric back to us. Believe me."

Nora patted Ellen gently on the back and whispered her thanks.

"Sweetie, sometimes life gives us troubles, but the Lord God always surrounds us with His peace and right now that's what I have to comfort me, His peace. I know my Eric is in a much better place now and I will see him again sometime soon. Ask God to grant you His peace my dear, He will do just that."

Nora held Ellen out at arm's length and wiped a stray tear from her cheek.

"I promise one day it will all make sense. As the pastor said, 'God's ultimate plan is beyond comprehension for us sometimes." Nora smiled through the grief that was clouding her eyes.

Ellen just nodded in response to the old woman's rambling. She didn't want to believe a word of it, but she would never argue with her. Ellen left Nora so that she could speak to the remaining guests and made her way down the hill to Jeremy. There was a luncheon scheduled at the church at noon, but neither of them felt like going to a celebration. It was a time to mourn the loss of their friend, not have a party without him.

Jeremy dropped Ellen off at her parent's home later that afternoon. She walked in the front door, thankful that her parents weren't home from the luncheon yet. Ellen didn't want to see or talk to anyone right now. She made her way back the hall to her bedroom and flopped on her bed. The emotions she had experienced that day had drained every ounce of energy from her body. All she wanted to do now was sleep the day away.

The next morning Ellen awoke with a start as the sun filtered through her bedroom blinds. She had somehow managed to sleep until 9am. The sun was a tease, trying to brighten a promising new day, but in reality, it was another nightmare without Eric here. Ellen wasn't sure if she would ever get out of this funk. Each day was like another slap in the face from reality, shouting at her, "Your best friend is gone for good."

She was thankful for Jeremy, her rock in this time of sorrow. They were going through this together and she knew one day they would overcome this and move on to a bright new future, even though that future seemed bleak right now.

Their school was closed for an in-service day, which was a welcome break as far as Ellen was concerned. This gave her and Jeremy a day together to spend at the beach, trying to regain some normalcy in their lives again.

Ellen got up and moved around her room, filling her drawstring bag with some necessities for their day trip. They were going to their favorite beach spot, about twenty minutes up the coast from her parent's place. Sandy Foot Cove was a special place they shared between the two of them, a place they had discovered when they first started dating. Eric had tagged along many times with them as well. Today they planned to place a small wooden cross that they had constructed together, in the sand dunes to commemorate Eric's significance in their lives.

Jeremy was right on time picking her up and she slipped quietly into the passenger seat. They rode together in silence the whole way to the cove; the emotions of the past week had exhausted both of them.

Jeremy pulled into the small parking lot that was situated across from the Sandy Foot Cove picnic area. Luckily, no one else was present, but this place wasn't a real big tourist area anyway.

Jeremy pulled Eric's cross from his trunk and turned to Ellen "Where do you think we should put it?"

"I think we should place it in the dunes closer to the shore, so that every time we come back here and visit we know right where it is. Plus, Eric would like to be closer to the shore. He loved it here." Ellen inhaled a deep breath, trying to keep her emotions at bay.

She and Jeremy walked for a few minutes down the shoreline to a spot where they would always sit and talk together. The area had multiple big, black rocks that jutted out into the ocean, waves crashing against them, filling the air with a salty mist.

They walked over to the dunes and began to dig a small

hole with the shovel Jeremy had brought. Then they placed Eric's cross gently in the soft sand. It was white with the words, 'To our forever best friend,' painted in blue across the front. Jeremy and Ellen stepped back to admire their work and then they each said a few words in remembrance of their dear friend.

They walked hand in hand down to the water when they were finished. Ellen slipped of her shoes and let the waves wash over her toes. The water was a little chilly, spring not having warmed it to a more pleasant temperature yet, but Ellen didn't mind. It was refreshing not only for her feet, but for her weary heart. They walked back and forth in the wet sand for what seemed like hours, filling their lungs with the soothing ocean air. Later on in the afternoon, they placed a blanket on the ground and ate the picnic lunch Ellen had packed earlier that morning.

"Ellen, I need to talk to you about something. It's not going to be easy, but I need to tell you now."

Ellen started to panic a little. Jeremy never talked like this before. After all they had been through recently did he need to dampen the mood even more with bad news?

"What is it?" Ellen hesitantly asked him.

"I can't see you anymore," he put out there bluntly. "All I can think about is the fact that I killed Eric, maybe not directly, but indirectly. When I'm with you all I can think about is him and the three of us together. I don't deserve this happiness. It's not fair to Eric."

"What?" Ellen resisted the urge to slap him. "Jeremy, what you're saying... no! This doesn't make sense! Jeremy I need you!" Ellen stood up, shouting at him. "You think this isn't hard for me too? I feel just as much a part of Eric's death as you do, but that doesn't mean I'm throwing everything else away! He wouldn't want this!" Ellen was in a fit of panic and tears now. How could this be happening?

"I'm sorry Ellen. This may not make sense to you, but I feel it's what I have to do, what I need to do. I already spoke to my parents about moving out to my uncle's place in Wyoming. I'll be getting a fresh start in life, working at his ranch, bettering myself. The plans are already in place and I move out there next week."

Ellen burst into heart wrenching sobs, unsure of what she could even say. Was this another terrible nightmare? How many nightmares could she handle at one time?

Jeremy went on, almost oblivious to the torment he was causing Ellen, "I think you should get away too, away from the pain of this place, the memories. It's not good for either of us to drown in the past, in the pain. Eric would want us to move on. We can always come back and visit, see the cross we placed for him."

Ellen couldn't take it anymore. She started running down the beach, farther and farther down the shore she went, until she couldn't hear Jeremy calling out her name anymore. She plopped down in the sand and buried her face in her hands. She was not leaving this place. She couldn't forget the memories here, yes, there was pain here too, but how could she preserve Eric's legacy if she just up and left him? Jeremy was being a huge jerk, not even caring about anyone's feelings. If he couldn't deal with his grief then he needed to admit it, not break her heart over it.

Jeremy eventually made it down the beach to where she was and sat down beside her, wrapping her up in a hug. "I'm sorry, I know this hurts. It hurts me too, even though you probably don't believe that. I promise this is for the best. I can feel it in my heart." Jeremy kissed her softly on the forehead.

Ellen didn't respond to him. She didn't want to spoil this

final moment in his arms. She didn't think this would ever happen. They had a future planned together; they were in love, the forever kind she had thought. They sat there together and watched the sunset. After it disappeared behind the edge of the ocean, they made their way back to his car by moonlight.

Again, the drive was in complete silence, but this time for a completely different reason. This day marked the end of what Ellen had thought was forever, the end of her first love.

~*~

When Ellen finished her story, she looked back at Ryan. His eyes were watery, filled with tears about to fall. Without saying a single word, he wrapped her up in his arms and held her. The tears fell freely for both of them. Ellen's from pent up remorse and sadness; Ryan's from the pain she had endured and suffered through. The thought of her going through something so horrific made him want to hold onto her forever, never wanting her to go through something like that again.

At that moment, he promised her something, "Ellie, I will be your forever. I will hold you through the tough seasons in life and rejoice with you in the happy, joy filled moments. I will never leave you. I promise you that with my life."

Ellen knew he meant it.

CHAPTER TWELVE

The night had proven to be emotionally draining for Ellen, but she was thankful. Katie was fast asleep when she walked into her dorm room later that night, just a few minutes before midnight. She plopped down on her bed and let out a deep sigh. Tonight had been just what Ellen needed. A huge weight had been lifted off of her shoulders now that Ryan knew her story. Yes, it had been hard reliving each traumatic detail, but the release of pain from her heart was worth it. She would always miss Eric and she couldn't allow herself to completely forgive the hurt and rejection Jeremy had caused, but with Ryan in her life, she saw a bright, shining future and she was ready to go after it.

She slipped into her purple, silky pajama pants and an oversized t-shirt and slipped underneath her covers. She needed to get some rest before the first day of spring semester classes started.

Sleep came quickly and easily for her, something she hadn't had in what seemed like years.

~*~

Ryan brushed his teeth and finished getting ready to knock out some Z's before classes tomorrow. Tonight had been something he had never experienced before. He had never cared this much about a girl. After hearing her heart-wrenching story, all he wanted to do was hold her and never let her go. From the first day that he had met her, in the cafeteria on campus, he knew she would be in his life forever. Ryan was falling hard for this girl and he knew after that tear filled evening that she was the one. He knew he was going to take things slow, Ellie needed that. They also both had careers they were trying to follow, his being quite demanding of his time. He knew deep down that it would all be worth it, because in the end Ellie would be his, forever.

He pulled his comforter up to his chin and closed his eyes, whispering a quiet thanks to God for bringing Ellie into his life.

~*~

The next two weeks flew by, filled with homework, class time and extra activities. Ryan would start spring training workouts soon, so he and Ellie planned to go on their first date this evening. It was an official date, finally moving forward from the friendship zone. Ellen couldn't help but feel excited. Ryan was special to her and she was ready to finally take the first step into a dating relationship.

Ryan had called and talked to her father asking

permission to date his daughter, which Ellen had found super sweet. Jeremy had never done anything like that before, and even though Jeremy had been a nice guy, he was nothing like Ryan.

Ellen chastised herself for comparing again. She needed to stop thinking about Jeremy and focus solely on Ryan. Jeremy was gone and Ryan was in her life now. She finished brushing her nutmeg-brown hair and did one last check in the mirror to make sure she looked her best. She smiled at her reflection, satisfied by her appearance, then made her way downstairs to meet Ryan. Ellen didn't know where they were going or what they were doing yet. Ryan had said it was a surprise and Ellen was really looking forward to it.

He leaned against his Jeep, smiling at her as she made her way out to the front of the dorm building. He was dressed in dark jeans with a white t-shirt that showed off his muscular frame. Ellen's cheeks grew warm at the sight of him. There was a reason every girl in the school wanted to date this guy. Lucky for Ellen though, he only had eyes for her and that made her feel special.

"You look beautiful," he said as he opened the Jeep's door for her.

Ellen smiled at him and hopped into the seat. "You look quite handsome yourself." She felt her cheeks blush again as she gave him the compliment.

He winked at her and made his way around the front of the Jeep to his door. It was a beautiful day for the beginning of February, unseasonably warm for this time of year. Ryan had removed the top of the Jeep and rolled down their windows. The wind whipped Ellen's hair around her face and she wrapped it up in her hand to keep it from getting too tangled. She enjoyed the breeze hitting her face and breathed in the fresh southern air.

They conversed about their week as they headed to wherever Ryan's surprise date spot was. Ellen was getting anxious to see where it was they were going to end up.

About forty-five minutes later, they finally pulled onto a dirt driveway with a sign that hung over it saying Heart and Soul Ranch. Ellen's curiosity peaked slightly wondering what they were doing at a ranch. It didn't look like a public place for people to visit, which confused Ellen. "What is this place?"

Ryan was beaming from ear to ear, "Well, my aunt and uncle own this ranch and I thought we could go horseback riding on the trails. Have you ever ridden a horse before?" He glanced over at her as he pulled his Jeep up to the large, rustic barn and shut it off.

"When I was a little girl I went to a camp where we rode horses, but that was a long time ago. I'll need my memory refreshed for sure." She was shocked that he had never told her about this place before.

"Don't worry; it's as easy as riding a bike."

He walked around to the front of the barn and Ellen followed behind him. She was a little nervous about riding a horse again, because if she remembered correctly the horse she rode when she was little hadn't been the friendliest. She trusted Ryan though and was more than willing to give it a shot.

Ryan waved hello to a man named George, one of the hired helpers she assumed, and made his way to the back of the barn where all the equipment was stored. "I'm going to grab what we need and get the horses ready to go. It shouldn't take me too long. If you follow me I'll introduce you to the horses we'll be riding today." He grabbed a saddle off of the wall and a few other things, then headed back down a row of stalls. Ellen followed right behind him until he stopped in front of a beautiful chocolate brown mare.

"She's beautiful," Ellen gasped. "What's her name?"

"This is Majesty. The horse you'll be riding today. She's got a gentle soul and you'll be best friends by the end of the day." Ryan started preparing her for the ride and Ellen reached out to pet her nose. The horse nuzzled right into her hand and Ellen's earlier worries vanished.

Ryan finished up with Majesty, led her out of her stall, and tied her up to an outside fence post. Ellen followed him to the next stall that housed a gorgeous, black stallion named Thor. Ryan got Thor ready to go and tied him to the same fence post as Majesty.

"Alright, are you ready to go?"

Ellen grinned. "Yep, let's do this!"

Ryan helped her mount Majesty, which was much easier then Ellen had thought it was going to be, and ran her through a quick tutorial of how to control the horse and a few simple commands. Once Ellen felt confident enough, Ryan mounted Thor and began to ride down a trail towards the back of the barn.

"There are tons of trails on my uncle's property, but this one is my absolute favorite and you'll see why when we reach the end."

Ellen steadied herself on the horse as she pulled up alongside Ryan, the farther they rode the more confidence Ellen exuded. After a few minutes, she felt like a pro.

"So, where were your aunt and uncle? I didn't see them when we were down at the barn."

"They're traveling around Europe right now, but they gave me permission a long time ago to visit whenever I want to take the horses out. I've been riding horses since I

76

was little and it's always been a time for me to get out into nature and just be thankful for the peace and tranquility. God's beauty radiates out here and it amazes me. Doesn't it amaze you?" Ryan turned to face her.

"Yes, it does." Ellen tried to hide her uneasiness about his mention of God. It wasn't a subject she wanted to delve into, so she just agreed with his statement.

Luckily, he didn't seem to sense her hesitation with his question and they continued down the wooded path. South Carolina was a beautiful state. On one end, you had the sandy beaches and on the other, you had these beautiful wooded forests.

The trees were still bare, winter not releasing its grip on them yet. They would be budding soon within the next few weeks, but even without their leaves, it was still a lovely sight to take in. The breeze filtered through the trees, tickling Ellen with a satisfying warmth. The fresh air filled her lungs and made her want to disappear into this moment forever. It was so peaceful.

They continued moving their horses forward, casually talking here and there between them. They were both satisfied in being silent at times and taking in their surroundings.

"We'll be at the end in a few minutes. I can't wait for you to see it." Ryan sped Thor up a little more and Ellen nudged her heel into Majesty, urging her to keep up. The horse responded and picked up the pace.

A few minutes later, as Ryan had said, they reached a clearing and the view Ellen laid her eyes on was simply spectacular. They were on the edge of a mountain that overlooked a valley below. It was like something pictured in National Geographic, yes, it was that gorgeous. They hopped off their horses and Ryan tied them both to a nearby post.

"I wanted to wait to bring you up here when the trees would have leaves on them, but I couldn't wait."

"Oh Ryan, it's beautiful just the way it is." Ellen looked out over the expanse of the trees below them and the sunny sky above them. "I'm not sure what to say, except it's so beautiful." The both sat down on a large, flat rock and just took in the scenery around them.

"I'm glad you like it. I come here as often as I can to remind myself how big the world is and that I'm just a small part in it. Keeps my head from getting too big." He chuckled to himself.

Ellen playfully smacked his arm. "I don't think your head would ever get too big. You're the most humble person I've ever met."

Ryan slid his arm around her shoulders and she slid closer to him. They sat there together and savored the moment, enjoying each other's presence.

"We should probably make our way back to the barn before it gets too dark," he said.

"Ok, if we have to. This place makes you want to sit here forever and never leave. Promise me we can come back sometime?" Ellen pleaded.

"Absolutely." He stood up and walked over to the horses, untying them from the post. Ellen missed the warmth of his body next to hers and reluctantly got up to head back to the barn.

Once they got back and got the horses situated Ryan asked if she'd like to stop at Gino's for some pizza before heading back to the dorm.

"You don't have to ask me twice. I'm starving!" Ellen exclaimed.

They downed an entire pizza between the two of them.

The adventures of the day had left them both ravenous. Ellen wasn't ready for this day to end and she tried to hold onto every moment for as long as she possibly could. Ryan made her feel giddy and happy, something she had been missing for a long time.

As nighttime overtook the campus and students began making their way back to their dorms, Ryan dropped Ellen off at the steps outside her building.

"I had a wonderful day. Thank you for spending it with me." He took a step closer to her.

"Thank you for taking me. I will never forget this day, Ryan." Her nerves started to creep up on her, fearing he was going to kiss her. The first kiss was always uncomfortable and nerve-racking, but luckily he wrapped her up in a hug and they avoided the awkward moment completely.

The strength of his embrace warmed her soul. She felt safe and secure in his arms, as if nothing wrong would ever happen again in her life, because she had Ryan. She took in one last whiff of his cologne before he pulled away, promising to text her later.

She stood on the bottom step and watched him drive away to his dorm across campus. Sighing, she turned and headed up to her room, reliving each moment of the wonderful day.

CHAPTER THIRTEEN

"I'm sorry ma'am there's no change." He grabbed his clipboard and walked back out of the room, leaving Ellen in the still silence. "No change." That's all the doctor ever said when he stopped in Ryan's room to check on him.

Ellen rolled her eyes as she watched the doctor leave. Sometimes she wished he would just keep his mouth shut when he checked on Ryan. What was the point in repeating himself every day? It did little to comfort Ellen and at this point, she knew there was no change in Ryan. She could see it every day she visited. She'd been in the hospital so often lately she was pretty sure she could do the doctor's duties herself.

She slid her chair closer to Ryan's bed and softly placed her hand on top of his. The only thing she took comfort in these days were the wonderful memories between her and Ryan that she had been reliving lately. They were so vivid; it was as if Ellen were traveling back in time to re-experience each one of them. If only she hadn't screwed up and ruined things between them. All these years they had lost together were such a waste, just thinking about it disgusted Ellen. Life would have been so different, more enjoyable, for both of them.

"Ryan," she whispered towards him, "I would give anything to go back and fix things or come back to you sooner. I wish you would wake up so I could look into your eyes and see that everything is ok, that nothing has changed between us." A single tear rolled down her cheek and dropped onto her hand. "Please, please give me a chance to make things right."

~*~

Their relationship grew stronger with each passing week and Ellen was on cloud nine. How had she been so blessed to have someone like Ryan in her life? It was truly a real life fairytale and Ellen was living it out.

They talked every day and spent time together when they could. Both of them remained focused on studies, not allowing each other to get distracted from their ultimate goals. Ryan had begun spring training camp, which took away from their time together in the evenings, but Ellen was beyond proud of his abilities and couldn't wait to see where this gift of his would take him.

It was late on a Saturday night, Ryan and she had enjoyed some time talking on a bench located in one of the common areas on campus. The easiness between them and the way conversation would continuously flow showed the strong bond between them. Everyone on campus knew how special the relationship was. There was no denying it, Ryan and Ellie were in love. Not the fake, movie kind of love, but the deep, emotional, unbreakable love that bound a couple together forever. Now, neither of them had shared this undeniable truth with each other, but it was there and it was breaking through like the sun on a brand new morning.

They both stared up at the moon, fingers entwined, the warm breeze softly stroking their faces. "I enjoy nights like these, especially when I have you next to me. I just wish I could hold on to moments like this forever." Ellen turned to face Ryan, keeping her hand in lock with his.

"I know exactly how you feel," Ryan turned on the bench to face Ellen. "I've never met anyone like you Ellie. You make me feel all warm and fuzzy inside and I know that sounds cheesy, but there is no other way to describe it."

Ellen giggled a tad, "I think it describes it perfectly."

Ryan became hesitant and his eyes held a seriousness that told Ellen what he was about to say was going to be extremely important. "Ellie, if I had known God was going to bring you into my life, I would have asked him to do it sooner. I want you in my life forever. The years you weren't in my life would have been better if you had been. I know we're young and people will say we don't know what we're doing, but I know I'm not wrong about this. I love you Ellie, and I will love you forever. I want to spend the rest of my life showing you just how much I love you." That's when he leaned in and kissed her for the first time. It was warm and tender, just as Ellen had expected it to be, but it was more than just that. It was sweet and caring, everything Ellen dreamed it would be, his way of showing his undying love for her.

Ellen reluctantly pulled away, her eyes glossing over with tears of happiness. "Ryan, I love you too."

Ryan's eyes lit up and he pulled her close, hugging her tightly. "I was hoping you'd say that."

They stayed in that embrace for a few minutes, thankful for each other and relishing in the love that flowed between them.

Ellen woke up the next morning with an indisputable grin, which prompted Katie to grill her with questions. "What's got you in such a good mood this morning?" Katie winked, knowing that Ryan was always behind Ellen's smiles lately and today was no exception.

"Ryan told me he loved me last night." Ellen squealed.

"Oh my gosh, Ellie that's great!" Katie rushed over and wrapped her friend in a hug. "You have no idea how happy I am for you. You deserve this." Katie squeezed her friend again.

The girls continued their squeal fest as Ellen recounted every detail from the magical evening. Katie wanted nothing left out about their first kiss, leaning forward and hanging onto every word as Ellen shared.

Ellen was so thankful with where her life was right now. She had a wonderful boyfriend, an encouraging and thoughtful best friend in Katie, supporting, loving parents and school was going really well. This wasn't cloud nine; this was cloud ten. After everything Ellen had gone through when she lost Eric and then Jeremy, she deserved some happiness. She was finally able to move forward.

CHAPTER FOURTEEN

"Ah, summer break, just what we need." Katie said as she threw the last of her belongings into her suitcase. "I'm going to miss you though, since I'll be in Colorado most of the time. I promise to come and visit if I ever have enough money for a plane ticket." She smiled over at Ellen, who was also loading her bag with the last of her things.

"Well, we'll talk every day. I'm sure of that." Ellen added.

"Oh, of course. There's no doubt about that." Katie zipped up her suitcase and placed it on the floor with the rest of her things. "Do you and Ryan have any plans for the summer? Rendezvous' on the beach? Late night make-out sessions at the park? Sleepovers?" Katie laughed at herself when she saw Ellen's cheeks turn a dark shade of red.

"Now Katie, you know we don't have a relationship like that. We are taking things slow and you know what Ryan's beliefs are, which lately I have been thinking aren't that bad at all. It's kind of nice thinking about saving yourself for marriage. It'll certainly make the honeymoon even more special." Ellen checked her phone to see if her parents had texted her about their arrival. Not yet.

Katie plopped down on the bed and stared at Ellen, "I don't mean to be super nosy or anything."

"Ha! We all know how nosy you can be Katie." Ellen pointed out to her.

"Well ok, yes, I can be nosy, but in this instance I'm being serious with you. Don't you think it would make the honeymoon awkward and weird? And since when did you two start talking about marriage?"

"First off, Ryan and I always talk about our future together. We plan on getting engaged after I finish school and we'll plan our wedding in the summer before the NFL season starts."

"Well, aren't you two super-efficient. But anyway, back to my other question... don't you think it would be weird?" Katie probed her again for an answer.

"Well, at first I thought it was strange coming from him. Nowadays you don't hear about guys willingly pursuing that. Growing up in a church I knew what God said about it, but I never took it to heart after abandoning the whole God thing." Ellen set her suitcase on the floor next to the rest of her stuff and sat on her bed across from Katie, taking more interest in the ongoing conversation.

"Ryan is passionate about his faith, living it out every day, and I admire him for that. It's one of the qualities I love about him. No, I don't share his faith, but it works for us, because I support him in it and he doesn't pressure me to believe what he believes. Waiting until marriage is one thing he strongly pursues and I'm not going to be the one that takes that away from him. I can control myself and besides, we know we're getting married one day, so eventually we will have that kind of relationship and I think waiting is going to make it special." Ellen smiled as she thought about the future with Ryan. It was going to be amazing and she couldn't wait.

"Well, I'm glad you two are pursuing that together. It's admirable in today's culture. I just know that I couldn't do it, especially with someone as hot as Ryan is." Katie winked over at her friend and braced herself for the playful smack Ellen gave her.

"Hey that's my man you're referring to!" Ellen shouted.

"Girl, there is no denying the fact that you snagged yourself a good looking man. I just thought I would point it out to you, so you wouldn't forget."

Ellen smiled, "Oh, trust me, I know what I have."

Katie and Ellen burst into a fit of laughter and enjoyed the final few minutes together before both of them went their separate ways for summer break.

"Can I ask you a personal question before you go?" Katie queried as Ellen gathered up her things to meet her parents in the parking lot.

"Sure, what is it?"

"Did you and Jeremy 'do it' when you were dating? I mean, since you didn't embrace the waiting philosophy before and now you are with Ryan, I just wondered. You don't have to answer that... I didn't realize how personal that question was until I asked it."

"No, it's ok. I don't mind you asking." Ellen put her bag down and looked at Katie. "We were close once, but no, we never actually did it. We were alone in his parents' house, because they had gone out for dinner. We got into some things, but luckily they returned home before we went too far." Ellen blushed at the memory.

Katie shrugged, "Well I guess for your sake and Ryan's, it's good they got home before anything happened."

Ellen nodded. It had been awhile since she thought

about Jeremy and some of those feelings from long ago rushed back. Ellen pushed those thoughts and feelings aside, then went downstairs to meet her parents. It was time for summer break and she was ready.

Ryan was talking to her dad when she found them outside. He rushed over to her and pulled her into a hug. She dropped her bags and hugged him back just as tight. She was sad to leave him, but it would only be a few days before he came to visit. They only lived an hour apart so they would have plenty of time to spend together over the summer.

"I'm going to miss you." He kissed her softly on the cheek, both of them still reluctant to kiss in front of people, especially Ellen's parents.

Ellen whispered softly in his ear, "I'm going to miss you too."

They broke free from their embrace and Ryan helped her carry her bags to her dad's truck.

"You two seem to be getting along nicely." Ellen's mom commented, as she came over to give her daughter a hug.

"Yes, I love him a lot."

Meredith smiled, "Sweetie, it's so good to see you this happy." She gave her daughter a warm hug. "It reminds me of when your father and I first met and look where we are now." She glanced over at Colt, a loving admiration in her eyes.

"We only hope we can someday be where you guys are, mom." Ellen turned and watched the guys finish loading her things into the truck.

"I think someday you will be. I see the way you look at each other and it's special." Meredith stroked Ellen's back.

"Thanks Mom."

The drive home was uneventful and as soon as she

pulled into her parent's driveway, she sent Ryan a text announcing her safe arrival. He responded almost immediately saying he loved her and couldn't wait until they could see each other.

Ellen couldn't wait either. She wished she could fast forward time, that they were married already, and could be with each other all the time; but she had to be patient. It would happen eventually, until then, she needed to be thankful for the moments they had together.

CHAPTER FIFTEEN

Summer had been blissful. Ellen couldn't believe the last week of break had snuck up on her already. She didn't feel nearly ready enough to start classes again next week. Ryan was coming down to spend this final weekend together and Ellen was looking forward to it. Their relationship had blossomed into something beautiful over the summer and Ellen still couldn't wrap her mind around how lucky she was to have Ryan in her life. Ryan had already gone back to school two weeks ago to start fall training for the upcoming football season, so they hadn't had a lot of time to spend together since the end of July.

Ellen checked her hair one last time before heading out to wait for Ryan on the front porch of her parents' beachside cottage. This place would always be home for her, the coziness always brought her a sense of peace and belonging. When school or life in general became overwhelming, this place was where she always returned. Now that she deemed herself presentable, she stepped outside in her jean shorts and light, cotton t-shirt and waited for the arrival of her man.

All summer Ellen had been reluctant to take Ryan to

Eric's gravesite, but today she finally felt the need to allow him deeper into that part of her life. They were going to spend their morning at the gravesite, placing some roses on it and then later in the afternoon, they would head down to Sandy Foot Cove to see Eric's cross.

Ellen hadn't been to Sandy Foot Cove since the day Jeremy broke her heart, but she felt ready to go back, to start new memories with Ryan. She had wanted to visit on the first and second year anniversary of Eric's death, but had never mustered up the courage to do so. Especially with the tiny fear in her heart that somehow Jeremy would be there too, even though deep down she doubted it since he had moved out to Wyoming with his uncle.

She heard Ryan's Jeep rolling up the driveway, so she hurried and grabbed her beach bag off of the Adirondack chair on the front porch and made sure she had locked the front door. She waved to Ryan as she made her way towards his Jeep and climbed into the passenger seat. He gave her a quick kiss after she buckled herself in, lingering just a little. Ellen savored the salty taste of his lips, wishing she could kiss him forever. They had held true to their promise of waiting, even though at times Ellen found it extremely difficult to do.

"You look stunning as always," Ryan complimented her.

Ellen blushed, "Thank you." His compliments always made her smile.

Light conversation passed between them as Ellen directed Ryan to the cemetery. It was only about fifteen minutes from her parents' home.

"How was practice this week? Do you guys feel ready for the season?" Ellen asked after she directed Ryan to take a left onto a small side street.

"It went well for the most part. We definitely have some

small glitches to work out in our system, especially with some of the new guys coming in, but I'm feeling pretty confident in the team this year. Coach thinks we'll dominate the division just like we did last year, which excites me." Ryan turned right into the cemetery's entrance.

"Well that's really good to hear." Ellen directed him into a small parking lot. After getting out of his car, they began the walk up the hill to Eric's plot. "I'm looking forward to writing for you guys this season. Now that Sabrina graduated, Mr. Sharp has assigned all the football articles to me for the upcoming season." Ellen beamed from ear to ear with pride.

Mr. Sharp was the new professor in the journalism department and had been impressed with her work from last season. Ellen felt honored to take over her new duties. As a sophomore, it was uncommon, even rare to have headliners in the school newspaper, but she would do Mr. Sharp and the entire football team proud.

"Well, I personally will read every one as soon as it's printed or first-hand if you'll let me."

"We'll see about that." Ellen winked at him.

They crested the hillside and there was the tombstone with Eric's name etched across the front. Below his name were his date of birth and death and a loving tribute claiming what a dear friend he had been to everyone who had been part of his life.

Ellen took in a sharp breath as the memory hit her with full force again.

"Are you ok?" Ryan lovingly placed his hand on her back.

Ellen nodded as silent tears rolled down her cheeks. She dropped down to her knees and placed her hand on the stone. "Eric, I miss you so much." She rested her forehead on the cool marble and let the tears flow freely. She took in jagged breaths as Ryan knelt beside her and let her lean against him. She hadn't expected her emotions to hit her with such force. Ellen hadn't comprehended the toll the memories would take on her or that it would be this hard. She felt guilty in a way for neglecting Eric this long, but she was here now and that's all that mattered. Eric would have understood her reluctance to come here sooner.

Ellen drew strength from Ryan's presence and was thankful that he allowed her to remain quiet and process through her emotions. He slowly rubbed her back after he placed the roses at the foot of the stone for her.

After a little while, Ellen stood up and brushed the dusty soil from her knees. She placed a gentle kiss on Eric's grave and waved a quick goodbye, promising to come back again. Ryan took her hand and stroked her thumb as they made their way back to his Jeep. "You sure you want to go to the beach today too?" He held her door open for her and helped her up into her seat.

"Yes, it'll be good for me and I want to share it with you. It's rejuvenating in a way; something my soul needs to move forward in life." Ellen took in a cleansing breath, "Thank you for coming with me today."

"I wouldn't miss it. I want to be there for you through everything, even your past. If I can help you work through it then I feel it makes our relationship that much stronger." He kissed her hand softly before shutting her door and making his way to the driver's side.

They rode in silence to the beach, except for the occasional directions Ellen would give him. She was still processing through her emotions and Ryan was letting her work through it in her own time.

They pulled into the Sandy Foot Cove parking lot, which was thankfully mostly empty. They chowed down on some sandwiches Ryan had packed for them before exiting the Jeep and then made their way down to the shore.

Ellen reached for her beach bag and took another quick breath. The emotions today were taking over, but she needed this moment, especially with Ryan.

They walked hand in hand until Ellen found a good place to set up the bright orange beach blanket. They sat down and watched the waves crash onto the shore. Ellen sunk her toes into the sand, enjoying the coolness and working up the courage to walk Ryan down to Eric's cross memorial. The memories of the day Jeremy broke her heart rushed over her, but she tried not to let it consume her. She was here with Ryan now and their future was bright. Jeremy was her past and today was the day she would move on forever.

"I think I'm ready now." Ellen mustered up her courage and grabbed Ryan's hand, pulling him up off the ground and guiding him towards the dunes.

~*~

The warmth of Ellen's hand sent shivers up his spine. Her presence always enticed him, filling him with a passionate fire, which took everything in him to control. Not only was she beautiful, but she was sweet and caring. The girl Ryan had always prayed for when he was growing up was right here beside him. He was more than grateful that God had blessed him with Ellie. She didn't share in

93

his faith, which for most people would be a red flag, but slowly he saw God working in her heart. He knew one day she would see the light and come back. He never pressured her, but instead lived his faith out daily to show her God's light in his own life.

He followed Ellen up the dunes and that's when he caught a glimpse of the painted white cross in the sand. The tears started falling down Ellen's face again and she took in shallow breaths. Ryan wrapped her up in his arms and enjoyed the weight of her body pressed in against him. His own eyes started watering as he processed his own emotions, knowing how much it took for her to share these intimate moments of her past with him. He felt honored that she was that comfortable around him to allow him into this private part of her life.

The breeze picked up a little bit, lifting the coconut aroma from her hair to his nose. The sweet scent was tantalizing and it warmed his heart.

They stood there in each other's arms, viewing the cross and taking in this moment together. Ryan had a sudden, burning desire to propose to her right then, but he squelched that idea quickly. Now was not the time and deep down he knew neither of them were truly ready for that step. He kissed the top of her head and pulled away, wiping the tears from under her eyes. "I love you, you know that right?"

"Of course I do." Ellen stood on her tiptoes and kissed him. "I love you too."

She grabbed his hand then and they walked back down to the blanket in the sand. The sun was beginning to set and Ellen leaned her head on his shoulder as they cuddled close. Ryan closed his eyes and silently thanked God for allowing this day to happen. He would never forget it, just like all the moments he had with Ellie. They would be etched in his mind for eternity, because this girl was going to be his forever.

CHAPTER SIXTEEN

It was the first home game of the season and Ellen was pumped. Katie joined her in the press area with a Pepsi in her hand, bobbing up and down with excitement.

"There's your man," she pointed out. "I still don't know how you managed to snag him." Katie jabbed her in the arm.

"Some days I really don't know how I got this lucky either." Ellen continued to watch Ryan warm up, jotting notes down and preparing the outline for her article. Last week's story, their first away game, had been a hit and now that she was the lead on the football section of the school newspaper, she was able to travel to the away games with the team.

The atmosphere was electric as all the students and South Carolina fans came to celebrate their season's home opener. It was going to be an exciting one; Ellen could feel it.

They were playing against Georgia, a team that was picked to be in the top three in the country. Even with Ryan leading the way, the experts pegged South Carolina to only get as high as number ten in the country. Many of their playmakers from last season had been seniors, so they had lost a lot of talent, but Ellen knew Ryan was going to prove people wrong. He would prove that they weren't only good, but that they were better then the top projected teams.

The teams headed back to their respective locker rooms and prepared themselves for the game. Ellen would have access to the locker room directly after the game in order to conduct some player interviews to incorporate into her column; something she had never done before. She was a little nervous; interviewing people was not exactly in her comfort zone, especially because she didn't know many of the players very well. However, this was a part of the field she was studying. Now was as good a time as any to start preparing herself for the real world.

A few minutes later the players emerged and the captains made their way to the middle of the field for the coin toss. Georgia won the toss and opted to kick-off first, giving South Carolina the first crack on offense.

Ellen watched as Ryan slid on his helmet and jogged onto the field. Her heart warmed at the sight of him, but she tried to keep her mind focused on the game. No one was going to read an article about a journalist gushing over the school's quarterback.

The first snap of the game was a handoff to Tavian Miller, who tumbled forward for a gain of four yards. Ryan then stepped into the hurry-up offense, trying to keep the defense off guard and get an advantage early in the game. It seemed to work well for them as Ryan marched the team down the field with ease, capping the drive off with a seven-yard touchdown pass to rookie, Ethan Banks. The defense held their own against Georgia's strong running game keeping them off the scoreboard on their first drive.

Ellen continued to cheer as the South Carolina offense once again marched down the field for another score. Tavian Miller ran it in from the twelve-yard line, dragging two Georgia players along with him.

Towards the end of the second quarter, Georgia managed to put some points on the board and went into the locker room with some momentum. The score at the half was 17-10, South Carolina.

Ellen excused herself from the press area and made her way down to the food stands for a bottle of water. The heat was intense today and Ellen wiped some sweat from her brow, enjoying the refreshing coolness of the water as it hit the back of her throat.

She zigzagged back through the maze of students as she made her way towards her seat next to Katie, who was chatting with a handsome boy a few rows up from them. Ellen watched as Katie wildly threw her hands about, apparently in an intense conversation with the boy. Ellen chuckled to herself as Katie's antics attracted the eyes of quite a few people around her.

Ellen took another sip of her water and went over her first half notes before the second half started. It all looked good and she felt confident with what she had so far.

The players once again jogged out to their team benches and prepared themselves for another thirty minutes of football. Ryan blew a kiss in her direction as he made his way out of the tunnel and Ellen returned the gesture. He winked at her and turned his attention to the clipboard in his hand.

Georgia started the half with a fire in them, easily maneuvering right down the field and scoring, tying up the game. Nothing to fear though for the South Carolina fans, because Ryan also came out with a fire, completing each of his eight passes during the drive, including a deep throw to Isaac Woodley, which allowed the walk-in touchdown.

The game continued to go back and forth, but thanks to Ryan's late game heroics South Carolina pulled the upset win over Georgia.

The fans roared in excitement as the team gathered in the center of the field for a celebration. Ryan snuck out of the huddle and made his way over to Ellen behind the team bench.

"The win today was dedicated to you," he kissed her, the sweat dripping from his face, but Ellen didn't mind. She returned his kiss fervently. "Actually, every win this year I'm going to dedicate to you, because you are my inspiration," he said as he slowly pulled away.

Ellen waved her notebook, "And you sir are the inspiration behind this." She smiled up at him, the sunlight reflecting in his eyes.

He kissed her again and turned to head back to the team. "Dinner tonight at eight?"

"Absolutely!" She hugged her notebook to her chest and watched as he made his way back to the huddle. A warmth bubbled in her stomach, like a million butterflies trying to find their way out.

Ellen gathered up her belongings and headed down to the locker rooms to get a couple player interviews for her article.

~*~

The evening passed by much too quickly for both of

them as Ryan prepared to walk Ellen up to her dorm. They shared some secret kisses on one of the more private benches outside the building, trying to avoid prying eyes from passing students.

"I love you," he whispered against her ear. His breath tickled and she suppressed a giggle, trying not to spoil the moment between them.

Instead, she nuzzled against his neck and whispered her response of "I love you too."

They sat in each other's arms for a few more minutes before Ellen had to make her way up to her room. Neither wanted to end this moment together, but unfortunately life and schoolwork got in the way of what could be endless moments together.

Ryan leaned back and took her hands in his, "I wasn't going to say anything quite yet, at least until I had a few more details figured out," he brushed a loose curl from her face, "but I can't hold it back any longer. It's too exciting to keep from you." Ryan was grinning from ear to ear.

Ellen's heart pounded in anticipation, eager to hear what he was about to tell her, "What is it Ryan?"

CHAPTER SEVENTEEN

Ryan was having a hard time suppressing his excitement, but he needed to slow down so he could explain everything to Ellen. Then she could completely understand what was going on.

"Coach told me there was a scout there today watching the game. Apparently, there has been some interest in me earlier than expected and scouts are going to be watching my game films and attending games. If I generate enough interest, I can enter the draft a year early and be playing in the NFL at this time next year. Ellie, isn't this awesome news?"

"Ryan that's amazing! I'm so happy for you!" Ellen leaned forward and hugged him tightly. "I know you've been dreaming about this for a long time and it's great to see your dream coming true." Ellen smiled up at him, her brown eyes shining. The admiration she had for him made his heart beat faster. Having someone in his life that made him strive for bigger and better things, pushing him towards his dreams was amazing. He wasn't sure what he would do without her.

They sat there and talked a little longer before Ellen had

to go up to her room to finish studying for an upcoming exam. They exchanged a quick kiss goodnight and Ryan left feeling an unbelievable amount of love in his heart. He whispered a quick prayer of thanks that Ellen was in his life, as he always did after one of their dates and drove across campus to his dorm room.

He opened the door to his room to find his roommate, Alex, head banging to some music as he tried to study. Ryan gave him a quick wave to grab his attention and then Alex slid his headphones off.

"Hey man, out with Ellen again?" he asked.

"Yes, I was. I had some exciting news to share with her."

"You proposed?" Alex sat straighter on his bed, clearly more into the conversation now.

Ryan chuckled, "Not yet, man. Not yet. It's a little too early and she still has a lot of school left to finish."

The disappointment on Alex's face amused Ryan. Everyone on campus it seemed was ready for the two of them to move forward. "Well then, what did you discuss with her if you're still too chicken to ask her to marry you?"

Ryan threw a pillow at him as he sat down on his bed.

"Dude, I'm kidding." Alex tossed the pillow back to Ryan. "Seriously, what did you talk to her about?"

"I found out there was a scout at the game today and they are looking to see if I can enter the draft early. That means this time next year I could be playing in the NFL." Ryan was beaming with pride. All of his hard work over the years was finally paying off and propelling him forward.

Alex's eyes grew wide as the realization hit him. "Dude, that's freakin' awesome! Just think, next year I can say things to people like 'yeah that guy was my roommate in college.'"

Alex slapped Ryan's outstretched hand and brought him in for a hug. "I'm so stoked for you man. If I had to choose anyone that deserved this it would definitely be you."

"Thanks man." Ryan patted his friend on the back and sat back down on his bed. Alex went back to his music.

Ryan leaned back against the wall and stared up at the ceiling. There would be some things to work through with Ellen since this wasn't their original plan. Ellen would still have two years left of school when he entered the draft next spring, which would cause a long-distance relationship for them. They were strong though and Ellen was so supportive that Ryan didn't worry too much about it. They would make it through.

Ryan grabbed the playbook off of his desk and looked over some game planning. He needed to be sharp this season if he wanted to become a top NFL draft prospect.

~*~

Katie was out with some other friends to celebrate the win when Ellen walked into their room. She was thankful for the quiet time she had to herself to contemplate the news Ryan had just shared with her. It was exciting for sure and Ellen was beyond happy for him, but she had some slight reservations about it. How would their relationship change with him leaving a year earlier than planned? Would they manage long distance well or would it cause some problems between them? Hundreds of questions swirled through Ellen's mind, but she tried to quiet her thoughts. No use worrying about something that hasn't happened yet. It would just add unnecessary stress. Besides, she and Ryan would have plenty of time to discuss and figure everything out before he was drafted. Ryan loved her and that's all that mattered. They would make it through anything together, Ellen was sure of it.

Finally calming herself down she reached for her sports' science book and began to study for her exam. The class was proving to be challenging so far this semester, but Ellen enjoyed it.

An hour and a half later, Ellen began to have trouble keeping her eyes open. She sat her book back down on her desk and slipped into her pajama pants. Katie had texted her and said she would be back around midnight and Ellen really wanted to stay up and share the news with her. She walked into the bathroom and splashed some cold water on her face, trying to wake herself up.

A few minutes later Katie burst into the room, singing a song to herself.

"Oh hey, I thought you would be asleep by now. You usually aren't up this late." Katie slipped her shoes off and tossed them onto the floor. She pulled out her ponytail and ran her fingers through her tangled, blond hair. "So, what's got you awake this late? Ryan?"

Ellen grabbed a water bottle out of the mini fridge for herself and tossed Katie one as well. "I have some exciting news to share with you!" Ellen twisted the cap off of her water bottle and took a sip.

Katie, mid-sip, spat out her water, leaped off of her bed and grabbed Ellen's hand. "Oh my gosh, you're engaged!" She glanced down at Ellen's naked finger and pouted, "Or not..."

Ellen wiped up the water that Katie spewed across the floor from her outburst and laughed. "I'm sorry to disappoint you, but that's not the news. Not yet anyway."

"Dang, I was really excited there for a second. What's your news then?" Katie sat back down on her bed.

"There was a scout at the game today watching Ryan. It looks like he is going to be able to enter the NFL draft a year early!"

Katie clapped her hands together. "Oh that's super awesome!" Katie jumped up and hugged her friend, then sat down beside her. "I bet Ryan is excited." Katie clapped her hands together again and inhaled sharply, "You'll be able to say you're dating an NFL quarterback! How awesome is that!" Katie squealed.

Ellen let that reality sink in. That would be pretty awesome.

The two of them continued to talk through the night, brainstorming endless ideas for the future. Katie was a treasure in her life and in moments like these, Ellen was grateful for her exuberant friend. Life would certainly be dull without her in it. Ellen's nerves had calmed down significantly after Katie reassured her that if anyone could get through a long-distance relationship it would be Ryan and her.

Ellen went to sleep that night with a full heart.

CHAPTER EIGHTEEN

The next few months flew by as Ryan embraced the new national attention that had been surrounding him. He was thankful for his agent Michael Armen who was able to help him through the interview preparations, the media and the pressing questions from NFL teams.

At times Ryan was so overwhelmed he wasn't sure he was going to be able to move forward, but God always provided him with a few quiet moments to just think, reflect and rest. He and Ellen had grown closer during this experience even though their time together had been limited to once or twice a week. He was so thankful for her support and encouragement. She was another reason he was able to make it through the crazy, intense weeks.

He knew deep down that all of this overwhelmed her too, but she handled it well. The long distance relationship was going to be a challenge, but luckily the team showing the most interest in him was Carolina and that would only be about a four and half to five hour drive between them. He would be busy with training camps, workouts and of course, the games when the season rolled around, but he had confidence in their relationship and that God would be with them through all of this.

The draft was coming up soon and Ryan was doing everything he could to prepare himself. His agent was a tremendous help. He had taken the spring semester off to do a lot of traveling, visiting potential teams. He planned to work hard over the summer to finish out his junior year and eventually, down the road, he would finish his business degree. It would be difficult to accomplish, to say the least, but Ryan was motivated and confident that he could do it.

The University of South Carolina was on spring break right now, so he and Ellen had made plans to enjoy some time together before the draft. He had a flight to New York on Wednesday and the draft officially started Thursday, continuing through the weekend. Carolina had the eighth pick in the draft, which is where he was going to end up his agent, Michael, had informed him. Ryan was excited. Carolina had had a difficult season; many key injuries had hindered their ability to win games. They were in need of a young quarterback to lead their offense and Ryan was ready to work with them. Carolina could turn into a very explosive offense with him at quarterback.

Ryan's phone rang and he quickly answered it. Michael was calling to give him his final travel details and to make sure Ryan had everything together that he needed. "You've got this, Ry-man." The nickname, 'Ry-man,' his agent had insisted on calling him hadn't thrilled Ryan at first, but it had grown on him over the past few months. "You'll make great strides on the NFL level. Promise me you'll keep me by your side and I'll make sure good things come your way. Got it?"

"Yeah Mike, got it."

Ryan finished his conversation with his agent, anxious to

leave to go pick up Ellen. They were having a sunset picnic on the beach to enjoy this final, quiet evening together.

~*~

Ellen sat on her parent's front porch, eagerly waiting for Ryan's arrival. She was very happy they were getting this time together before he left for the NFL draft. She was grateful that Carolina was drafting him, because it made the distance between them shorter. It also gave Ellen confidence that their relationship would survive the long distance test. She was ecstatic for Ryan, this was his dream and he was achieving it. It made her proud to be the girlfriend of an NFL quarterback. All these emotions ran through her on a daily basis, and sometimes it was exhausting, but Ryan kept her grounded.

She looked up as his Jeep pulled into the driveway and she ran to greet him. He kissed her softly and she savored the taste of his lips. It would be so difficult for her not to see him, but she could do it. They would be married someday soon and then she could look back on this time and realize it hadn't really been that difficult.

She stayed in his arms for a moment longer before they headed to the beach for their picnic. He excitedly shared all the new information he had about his travel itinerary and the draft. Ellen and her family unfortunately were unable to attend the draft, so she would have to watch it from home, but Ryan planned to come down to visit a week afterwards.

They cruised the beach highway, the salty ocean air awakening her senses. She could never get enough of this.

The sea had a soothing quality that calmed her soul every time.

They found a good spot to set down their blanket and dove into their picnic meal. Ryan packed homemade potato salad that his mom had made and some chicken ceasar wraps. It wasn't anything fancy, but this is what they enjoyed when they could. Simplicity.

The sun began to set as they enjoyed their food and time with each other. The sky transformed into a blended beauty of reds, oranges and yellows. Ellen leaned into Ryan as they watched the sun give way to the stars. Ellen started to worry that they would never have a moment like this ever again. She was concerned that the changes that were coming would squander these moments and they would never have opportunities like this, but Ryan slid his arms around her and pulled her tighter. "I know you're worrying, but please don't. Everything will be okay as long as God is a part of this." Ellen had started going back to church with Ryan, trying to become a part of the faith he lived out. It wasn't as horrible as she had thought and most times she actually enjoyed it, but mostly because they were getting time together in the midst of his busy schedule.

Ellen snuggled into him as his words washed over her. "I love you Ellie. More than you'll ever know. The time that's coming with be difficult to maneuver through, but we will get through it. I promise. I could never leave you and no matter what, I will make you my wife one day then we can walk this life together, side by side."

He turned and kissed her. A soft kiss at first that slowly turned deep and passionate. A kiss that proved every word he had just said. Ellen savored every second of it. It became desperate, a longing between the two of them to stay here in this moment. Ellen ran her fingers up his back and into his hair, massaging his head. Ryan easily slid his hands down to her waist, grabbing her hips and pulling her closer to him. Their kiss became deeper, more heated and Ellen didn't want to stop. A soft moan left his lips as he pulled away. Ellen sighed slightly, not wanting to stop, but she knew not to pressure him into more.

He kissed her again and whispered, "I love you Ellie and one day soon I will show you that." He winked at her.

Ellen grabbed his hand, "Ryan, I'm not sure how much longer I can wait."

"Me either," he said, still out of breath.

They leaned back in the sand and watched the stars twinkling in the night sky. The air had grown a little cooler, but Ellen wasn't cold. She was heated by her burning desires and was doing everything in her power to still her racing heart. She wanted to do more; she wanted to give all she had to Ryan, but she loved him too much to compromise his beliefs about waiting for marriage, so she took a deep breath. She could wait; Ryan was worth it.

Ryan grabbed her hand as they continued to watch the sky. He softly rubbed her thumb and talked about their future together. Ellen was content at this point and knew they would be okay. For now.

CHAPTER NINETEEN

It was draft day and Ellen was thrilled for Ryan's next adventure. It would take a toll on their relationship, but Carolina wasn't too far away. Ellen couldn't wait to see Ryan walk across that stage, hold up his jersey and have the hat of Carolina placed on his head. She wished she could be there to be part of this moment with him.

Ellen sat in her parent's living room, along with many of their neighbors and family friends. Most of them had met Ryan when he was in town visiting with Ellen and all of them were very excited for this moment.

Meredith had prepared a feast, as she always did when people were over. Being a host was one of her gifts and she always made everyone feel right at home. Ellen curled her feet up under her as she leaned into the corner of the couch. She took in the hustle and bustle around her, catching bits of conversation here and there. She was mentally prepared for this day, she knew what to expect and what was going on, but the way her heart felt was a different story. This was a big step in her relationship with Ryan and the doubts were creeping into her heart again. Ryan was usually able to squelch those fears, but since he wasn't here, it was a lot harder to keep them under control.

Ellen tried to listen to the reporters on the screen talking about the draft prospects and any surprises they thought would come up. The predicted number one pick was Tavon Banks, a running back from the University of Pittsburgh. Detroit was looking to lock him in with the first pick of the draft. Ellen listened for Ryan's name, which the reporters finally got too. She beamed with pride when his picture flashed across the screen and some highlight film was played.

"Carolina is looking to pick up this phenomenon out of the University of South Carolina and I believe he is truly a perfect match for their offense."

"I agree Tom, with his vision in the pocket and strong arm I can see him making a name for himself in the NFL. I think Carolina is making a very smart choice if they follow through and add him to their roster."

Ellen continued to listen to them go on and on about Ryan's abilities, pride shining in her eyes.

"He's going to be something special." Ellen's dad sat down next to her. "Are you ready for this?" Colt turned to his daughter, looking her in the eyes, making sure she was okay.

"I can't lie. I am nervous, but I know Ryan loves me and I know this is just the next step towards our future. Plus, I can't help but to be proud of him for chasing his dream. I would never want to be the person that held him back from that."

Colt took his daughter's hand in his and smiled. "Sweetheart, you two were meant for each other. Your mother and I can see that. We pray for you both every day and if you ever need anything you know that you can come to us."

Ellen leaned on her dad's shoulder and let out a sigh of pent up emotion. "Thank you daddy. I know I'll always have you and mom." She stayed in his arms for a few more seconds.

The NFL commissioner stepped up to the podium and began his speech, initialing the start of the draft. Ellen's heart began to race with excitement. This was it. This was the start of a completely new world for her. Everyone in the room quieted down and took their seats.

As expected, Detroit drafted running back Tavon Banks with the first pick. The young man made his way to the stage, waving to the crowd. He shook the commissioner's hand and gladly accepted his Detroit hat and jersey. Carolina had the number eight pick, so Ellen still had some time before her man walked across the stage. Each team had ten minutes to make their decision and most teams took the full-allotted time. If there were any trades made then the clock would start over for that team, so it would probably be about an hour and a half before Ellen saw Ryan.

The teams continued to pick up the players they wanted and before Ellen knew it pick number eight flashed on the board. Carolina's emblem appeared on the screen and the clock began counting down from the ten-minute mark. The commentators began talking about Ryan again and how great a fit he was going to be in Carolina's offensive scheme.

"What's taking them so long to announce their pick?" Ellen asked. "We all know they want Ryan."

"I'm sure they are just getting everything in order." Colt patted his daughter's arm, reassuring her that everything was fine.

San Diego's emblem flashed across the screen. "It looks

like there's been a trade!" one of the commentators exclaimed. "I wasn't expecting them to move up."

The other commentator responded, "It looks like they gave Carolina their second round draft pick and a first round pick for next year, allowing them to move up. I heard they were looking at the wide receiver from LSU. I guess they wanted to make sure they got him, before anyone else did."

The commentators continued to talk about the trade that was made, discussing their thoughts on it. Ellen's nerves were on edge and her father gently squeezed her hand. "Don't worry sweetie, it just looks like Ryan won't be picked up until the sixteenth pick now."

Because Carolina had traded to San Diego it moved them back a few spots, but it still looked like everything would work out since talk was that San Diego wanted Miles Rhode, the wide receiver from LSU.

"It looks like San Diego's pick is in."

The commissioner strode up to the podium and gave the announcement. "With the eighth pick of the NFL draft San Diego selects, Ryan Salas, quarterback out of the University of South Carolina."

The crowd roared in cheers on the television screen and the commentators immediately began talking about their surprise on the selection. "I didn't see this coming Tom. San Diego wasn't in the market for a quarterback, but I guess they saw how special this kid is and wanted to snatch him up."

"I agree Rick, this kid is truly something special and any team would be lucky to have him on their roster."

The commentators went on about the surprising pick, but Ellen tuned them out. "Wait what? NO! NO! This isn't right! Carolina wants Ryan!" Ellen was in a panic shouting

114

at the television screen. She watched as he crossed the stage, smiling and waving at the crowd. He shook the commissioner's hand and held his San Diego jersey up. Tears burned the back of Ellen's eyes, but she refused to cry in front of all these people. She turned and ran from the room, not wanting to see anyone. Her mom and dad called after her, but she just kept going. She grabbed her keys and headed outside to her car. She wasn't sure where she was going to go, but she had to leave.

Did Ryan know? And if so, why didn't he tell her? Everything was all wrong now. He couldn't go to San Diego. That wasn't their plan. The tears flowed freely now, blurring her vision. She hopped on the highway and drove to Sandy Foot Cove. Right now, she needed to be alone to process everything. It was dark outside, but Ellen didn't care. She felt the ocean calling to her, pulling her to her calm place, which is where she needed to be.

She pulled into a parking spot and walked down to the shore. She laid the large blanket she always kept in her car down on the ground and sat. The moon reflected off the waves bathing everything around her in a luminescent glow, but her heart was dark. How could Ryan have let this happen? He had to have known something. Why didn't he at least try to give her a heads up that there was talk about San Diego? Instead, she was left to be stunned in front of family and friends.

She hugged her knees to her chest, contemplating what in the world they were going to do now. Ryan was coming to visit next week and they would talk then, but Ellen felt hopeless. How were they going to make a relationship work if he was going to be clear across the country playing professional football?

The sound of the rushing waves crashing on the shore

helped calm her mind, but her heart was in a million pieces. Her chest hurt just thinking about what was coming next.

Soft footsteps made their way through the sand towards her. She figured it was her dad wanting to console her, but she was in no mood to talk to anyone right now. "I'm sorry dad, but I don't want to talk. I just want to be left alone."

"Ellie, it's me. I didn't expect to see you here."

Ellen's heart slammed against her chest at the sound of his voice. She turned slowly and looked up into his eyes. "Jeremy, what are you doing here?"

CHAPTER TWENTY

Three years had done him well. His eyes sparkled in the moonlight and his beard gave him a ruggedness that caught Ellen's eye. That voice had stirred up some emotions that Ellen had buried long ago, or so she thought. He stood there with his hands in his jean pockets waiting for an invitation to sit down.

Ellen gestured to the blanket allowing him to sit next to her. The heat she felt when he positioned himself beside her was overwhelming. His presence flustered her and she was trying her best to sort through her emotions quickly before she said or did anything stupid.

"To answer your question, I'm here for a few days visiting my parents. Tonight I'm here because I wanted to see Eric, to tell him what's been going on in life." He stared wistfully out towards the sea, his legs pulled up against his chest, just as Ellen's were. It was as if they both were trying to close off their emotions, keeping them locked up tight and refusing to release them. They both stared out towards the black horizon, a few stars dotting the empty space. The moon reflected in both of their eyes, shining a light on a past that had never had any closure.

Jeremy turned to face her, but Ellen refused to look in his eyes. She wasn't ready for this; she was vulnerable and confused, unsure of what to do. "I'm sorry Ellie, for everything. I should have never ended things the way I did. I should have never abandoned you at a time when both of us needed each other. I made a mistake and I'm sorry for that. I know you probably don't care and you're probably still angry with me. I understand completely, but Ellie I loved you. I loved you more than I cared to admit back then. I know we have gone our separate ways now and we are living different lives, but it was fate that you were here tonight, because I've needed to get that off of my chest for a long time. Would you please forgive me?"

His words were like a punch to the gut. Where was this Jeremy three years ago when she needed him? She didn't want to hear his sob story. The anger rose to her throat and it came out in a surge of pent up resentment and sobs. "Why now Jeremy? Why tell me this now? I don't care about what you have to say, because it's all pointless! I needed you back then and you abandoned me! You left me because you were upset and scared. If you truly loved me then you wouldn't have done what you did. You wouldn't have made me grieve Eric's death alone." She took a deep breath trying to control her sobs, "I can't deal with this right now." She stood and walked toward the edge of the ocean, letting the waves wash over her bare feet. It was cold, but it helped cool her emotions, allowing her time to think and process everything.

Jeremy walked up behind her and wrapped his arms around her shoulders. "Ellie, I did truly love you then. I thought I was doing what was best because I loved you, but obviously I was very wrong."

Ellen didn't pull away, because a part of her heart

needed his touch. She turned and buried her face in his chest, breathing in his cologne, the same one he wore in high school. She would never forget the smell of it. He rested his chin on the top of her head and let her cry, letting the past wash over her and allowing her to work through all of it.

They stood there for a long time before Jeremy led her back to the blanket where they sat down. Ellen wiped the final tears from her eyes; all the emotions had worked their way through her system. "I'm sorry for the outburst," she looked down at her toes digging into the sand, "You didn't deserve that. You were hurting just as much as I was back then. You just handled it differently than I did."

Jeremy continued to look straight ahead at the expanse of the ocean, "You didn't deserve what I did. I had no excuse for reacting that way." He turned to look at her and grabbed her hand in his. Ellen felt the spark, a spark that had never been extinguished from their past. She didn't pull away, allowing him to continue speaking. "Ellie, there are no words I can say to erase the hurt I caused you, but please know that if I could go back in time and undue it, I would, in a heartbeat."

The moment was becoming more intimate than Ellen could handle. She should tell him about Ryan, put space between herself and Jeremy. She should just walk away now, but the history between them, the one that never received proper closure was drawing her in like a magnet. His eyes locked with hers and Ellen didn't pull away when he leaned in to kiss her. A kiss letting her know how sorry he was. The warmth of his breath against her as he pulled away intoxicated her, filling her mind with the past and how much she had loved him. She should have stopped herself, but she lost control and leaned in again pulling him towards her and kissing him. He didn't protest and wrapped his hands in her hair, pulling her closer to him. A built up passion flowed between them that had been buried for three years and had never gone away.

Ellen sunk into his kiss, the comfort and familiarity of his presence driving her down a dangerous road. She knew she should stop, she was with Ryan, but her history with Jeremy was so strong that her long ago, teenage heart, took over complete control.

His hands glided over her body with ease and Ellen relished his touch. It was electric. His lips were soft and tender and she pressed into him harder wanting more. Jeremy responded to her, sliding his hands under her shirt and pulling it off of her. He laid her down on the blanket and nuzzled her neck, continuing to kiss her. Ellen pulled him down on her and continued to kiss him, tears running down her cheeks. She knew how wrong this was, but she couldn't help herself. She hadn't stopped loving Jeremy. She tore his shirt off and looked his body over in the moonlight. He had grown up; he wasn't the boy in high school anymore. She unbuttoned his jeans, as he undid hers and that's the moment she knew, she was going to make an unforgivable mistake.

~*~

Ryan hadn't known San Diego wanted him until Carolina had been up for their pick. It was a last minute decision between the two organizations and he had no way of contacting Ellie with the news. He knew she was going to be shocked and upset, but he had promised her they could get through anything and he was going to keep that promise.

After the party he attended last evening, when the draft festivities were over, he had tried calling Ellen a few times. She hadn't picked up, even after he left her two voicemails. He knew she was probably angry, but she would work through it. They would get through it together. After signing his rookie contract early this morning, he headed to a jeweler his agent had recommended.

It was a solitaire diamond, set in a white gold band and as soon as he saw it, he knew. It stood for the one true love of his life and the love that he knew they would share forever. He had already talked to Ellen's dad two weeks ago and had received the man's eager blessing. Her mother had shed a few tears, saying how thankful she was that Ryan was in their daughter's life. He paid the jeweler with the money he had just earned from his new contract and watched as the man engraved on the inside of the band, *"You are my forever."* Ryan had known those four words since he had laid eyes on Ellie that first day in the cafeteria.

The guy finished up with the ring and handed the box to Ryan and winked, "You are going to make that girl a very lucky lady."

"No sir, she's going to make me a very lucky man." He smiled and turned to walk out of the shop. He gently placed the ring in his pocket and strode back down the street to his hotel. All he could do was smile. He was going to make Ellie his forever and that gave him a reason to never stop smiling.

CHAPTER TWENTY-ONE

The hot water rushed over her as she tried to scrub off the guilt. She scrubbed so hard her arms felt raw, but nothing was going to take away the guilt and shame she felt. It consumed her. How had she let this happen? She let the heart from her high school past take over and now she had to live with something that would slowly eat away at her.

Jeremy hadn't said a word about their encounter other than a mumbled "I'm sorry," leaving Ellen with a tormenting shame. He had walked off into the darkness leaving Ellen on the beach hugging her knees to her chest. All she could do was rock back and forth and wish for time to rewind. Ryan didn't deserve this; Ryan didn't deserve someone like her. A deceiver, a cheater, worthless. The tears poured freely down Ellen's cheeks as the waves crashed on the shore, like they were trying to pound away at her guilty conscience to no avail.

Ellen hugged herself in the shower, willing the thoughts away. It had been almost a week since then and the shame Ellen felt was stronger now. Ryan was coming later today and she knew she had to tell him. She had to leave him now. He deserved so much better and the sooner Ellen let him go the better it would be for him.

She twisted the shower nozzle, ceasing the flow of water. All that was left was a room full of steam fogging the mirror and her mind. She had told Ryan that they needed to talk, but he assumed it was about his new move to San Diego coming up. Little did he know that heartbreak was on the near horizon and he wasn't going to see it coming.

Ellen swiped her hand across the mirror, allowing her reflection to stare back at her. Her eyes were red and puffy, matching her skin. She stared hard at herself in the mirror, angry at the girl that was about to break Ryan's heart. How could she?

The guilt had been so overwhelming the past few days that she finally broke down in her mother's arms and confessed. Her mom had been questioning her mood, knowing that something was eating away at her daughter. Meredith had held her and stroked her hair, allowing Ellen to spill her shame onto her shoulder.

She was supposed to return to school tomorrow. Spring break was officially over and Ellen was more than ready to go back. After the devastation today would certainly bring, she was going to need any and every kind of distraction she could possibly get. Diving into her studies would do just that.

Ellen checked her phone for the time as she dressed for the day. As she slid into a worn pair of jeans, she braced herself for what was coming. Ryan would be here soon and Ellen wished that this were all just some horrible nightmare. Unfortunately, she made an unforgivable mistake that she could never undo and her heart was broken beyond repair. She wasn't looking for sympathy from anyone and she knew she was going to have to own up to her stupid decision, but the fact that Ryan was going to be hurt is what was tearing her to pieces.

She heard his Jeep pull into the driveway and slowly made her way out onto the front porch. Her mom had nodded to her from the living room couch as she shut the front door, knowing what was in store for her daughter. Meredith had been disappointed and Ellen was fully aware of that, but her mom gave her full support in this next step and for that, Ellen was grateful. Her dad had come into her bedroom last night and talked with her as well, letting her know he was praying for her, knowing her next conversation with Ryan would be a difficult one. He had been disappointed as well, which tore deep into Ellen's core. Disappointing her dad was something she had never wanted to do. That alone was almost as heartbreaking as what she was about to do next.

She made her way towards Ryan as he enveloped her in a warm hug. "I've missed you so much. I know we have a lot to talk about, but can we wait until we get to where I'm taking you?" His eyes pleaded with her.

Ellen reluctantly agreed, not wanting to drag this day out, but she also wanted to savor these last few moments with him before she told him a permanent goodbye.

She plastered a smile on her face, trying to hide the emotions raging inside of her. Ryan didn't seem to notice, which was good. Anything to keep things normal between them.

He grabbed her hand while he drove and Ellen savored the feeling of his fingers between hers. Strong, secure, safe. Nothing like Jeremy. She mentally smacked herself. She had ruined things, ruined what was going to be a wonderful future with a wonderful man. All for nothing, absolutely nothing.

He pulled into Sandy Foot Cove about half an hour later and the pangs of guilt raced around in her mind causing her temples to throb. Why here? Out of all the places in the world, why had he brought her here?

It seemed like a cruel joke from God that He would allow her to break Ryan's heart in the very spot she had made her life-altering mistake. It was something she deserved she guessed. A harsh punishment handed down from God condemning her for her unforgivable sin. That's how He worked, right?

Ryan had a beaming smile across his entire face the whole time he led her down to the shore and all Ellen could think about was how quickly what she had to tell him would wipe it off of his face.

He took both her hands and looked into her eyes. An undeniable sparkle shone in his. "Ellie, I brought you here today because the many times we have shared on this beach together have made me fall more and more in love with you. To the point where I can't imagine living my life without you. You are my sunshine, bringing light into my life, even on the dreary days. You are my motivator, pushing me beyond my limits, pushing me to pursue my dreams. You are my angel, because I know for a fact that God put you in my life. I love you with all my heart."

Ellen's heart was racing. What was he doing? She had to stop him, but the words weren't forming. She had to open her mouth and try to keep him from continuing. The panic rose in her throat and her palms began to sweat profusely, as she realized what was happening.

"My Ellie, would you please do me the honor of being my wife? I know that there are uncertain things coming up in our lives, but we can make it through anything. Nothing can break the bond between us, not even the distance we'll have to endure for a short time. I will fight for you every day Ellie, until I see you walking down the aisle towards me. I promise you that. So, Ellie, will you marry me?" He lowered himself down to one knee, pulling a small, black box from his pocket. A beautiful solitaire diamond was nestled in the velvet.

Ellie choked on a sob as she realized the magnitude of pain she was about to cause. She reached for Ryan's hands and pulled him up. She had to do this now, as hard as this was going to be, she had to tell him and let him move on.

A wave of nausea built up in her throat, but she swallowed, pushing it down, along with her fear. "Ryan, I can't marry you."

She launched into her confession, her heart crumbling as Ryan's emotions crossed his face and turned into full-blown tears. She continued on, not allowing herself to stop until she was finished. He deserved to know the truth.

When she finally finished she turned and ran down the beach, her feet pounding the sand. Pounding out all her anger, her remorse, her guilt. None of it seemed to go away and the farther she ran the angrier she became at Jeremy and even more towards herself. Ryan called after her, but she refused to turn around, she refused to run back to him. She had to let him go. She called her dad asking him to pick her up at the pier. When she reached the boardwalk, she sent one final text to Ryan before shutting off her phone.

Please do not contact me. You have to move on Ryan. You deserve better. You deserve someone that would never do what I have done. Someone that will love you forever and never make the mistake that I have made. Again, I'm sorry.

She shut her phone off before he could respond. She saw her dad's truck pull into the parking lot and hopped into the passenger's seat. Colt rested his hand on his daughter's shoulder, giving her strength through his touch to get through this time.

~*~

What had just happened? Ryan's mind was spinning a hundred miles an hour, trying to wrap itself around Ellie's outburst. His emotions were all over the place and he was trying his best to process them. After spending some time standing there on the beach in disbelief he walked to his Jeep and got in. He rested his head on the steering wheel and punched the dashboard. He proposed to her and this is what he got? A confession that she had cheated on him? Yes, he was angry, but he loved her and had promised her that no matter what, they would get through anything together. He hadn't intended on going through this kind of trial, but God had a reason for everything and even though Ryan was heart-broken, he knew Ellie was deserving of his forgiveness.

Unconditional love. It's what God showed his people numerous times throughout the Bible, even after all of their rebellion and disobedience. No matter what they did or how many times they did it, God was quick to forgive and accept them again. God called Ryan to love like that and this was his chance. This was his chance to show Ellie the extent of his love and not only his love, but God's love. Was it going to be easy? No. However, Ryan knew what he had to do, no matter how long it took to get through to her.

He read Ellie's text message, but ignored it. She may feel

that he deserved better, but she was wrong. Ellie was everything he had prayed for in a future wife. No one was perfect; everyone makes mistakes. That's what forgiveness and reconciliation were for.

He drove to her parents' house later that night and Colt came out to greet him. Ryan shook hands with the man and asked to speak to Ellen.

"She doesn't want to talk Ryan and as her father I want to respect her decision. It hurts me to see her going through this and it hurts me knowing what it's doing to you. You are the man I've been praying for to be in my daughter's life." Colt swiped a tear from the corner of his eye. "Right now things may look bleak, but I know God placed you in her life for a reason."

Ryan looked Ellen's father in the eyes, "Sir, I feel the same way and I will never stop loving her. Can you please tell her that? Tell her everything I promised will always remain true, nothing has changed for me."

"I will." Colt pulled Ryan into a hug, patting him on the back. "If you truly feel that way then please don't ever stop pursuing her son. She needs you."

"I promise."

CHAPTER TWENTY-TWO

The memories still made her heart cringe in pain. No amount of time that passed could heal that wound. It was still open and oozing and all Ellen could hope for was reconciliation with Ryan, the man she had never stopped loving.

Her parents had made their way out to California to be with Ellen two days ago and they were all staying with her mom's sister, Charlotte. Her Aunt Charlotte had always been critical about every little thing and never easy to get along with. But during this time, Ellen was thankful that her aunt could keep her negative personality under wrap and be generous enough to let them stay with her for the time being. Ellen was glad to be saving money on a hotel bill, because even though she had a good paying job as a top reporter in New York, she still didn't want to spend her money needlessly.

It had been almost two weeks since Ellen had arrived here in San Diego to be with Ryan and there was still no change in his condition. Each day that Ellen walked into his room she felt her hope dimming a little bit more. How much longer could a person go on living like this?

Most of the time Ellen would be in the room with Ryan by herself for as long as she was allowed. Both she and Ryan's parents would be in and out throughout the day when they could, showing their support for her and also praying over Ryan. Whenever they would gather to pray Ellen would back into the corner and allow them their time with him. Obviously, it wasn't helping, so Ellen didn't see the point, but she respected their faith.

The fading sunlight streamed through the open curtain that evening, casting a hazy, orange glow on the magazine Ellen was looking through. She glanced over at Ryan, watching the steady rise and fall of his chest. The doctor said the scars on his face were healing nicely; better than they had expected, but all Ellen wanted was for Ryan to open his eyes. She wanted him to do that one simple thing so badly, it made her heart ache. She placed the magazine on the wooden stand next to Ryan's bed and stood up. She reached for his hand and held tight, willing life into him.

"Ryan, wake up for me please," she whispered. She lifted his hand to her face and brushed it against her cheek. A single tear rolled down her face when a nurse entered the room letting her know that visiting hours were over in ten minutes.

Ellen gently placed his hand back on the bed and gathered up her things. Her boss had been getting on her to write her next article and another message on her phone screen indicated his annoyance at her slow pace. She took one last look at Ryan before she walked out of the room and turned left towards the elevators down the hall. She had done a little bit of research and had some ideas for new articles, but with everything going on, she couldn't concentrate. She sent her boss a quick text as she rode the elevator down to the parking lot, saying she was working on something for him, trying to appease him for now. She was determined to finish her research tonight and start on her next piece. Yes, she was struggling right now with everything going on, but she couldn't lose her dream job that she had worked so hard for.

~*~

Ellen dove into her studies, trying to focus on everything but Ryan, the last few weeks. He had called her numerous times saying they could work through this, but Ellen didn't feel worthy of him anymore. He deserved someone so much better and she told him that more than once. The first few times she had answered him, but now she ignored him. She needed her heart to heal and he needed to let go and move on. He was starting a new career and he needed to focus on it. His calls came less now, the voicemails were fewer, and even though it tore Ellen's heart into pieces, she knew it was the best for both of them.

She had signed up for a summer semester, taking extra credits to propel herself to an earlier graduation next spring. Graduating a year early would save her a lot of money, plus, she could pursue her dream career as a sports journalist a little bit sooner. She already had an externship lined of for her fall semester as long as she passed her summer classes. She would be writing small articles for local sports' teams in Columbus, South Carolina and the beauty about the externship was that she could work on everything from home and have no travel worries.

Her primary focus was football and with this externship she would be working on sports like basketball and baseball as well, which would help with her resume. It was one-step closer to her dream of reporting for the NFL.

She turned back to her studies, snapping herself out of her daydream and buckling down to focus on passing her finals. She would have two weeks to relax in between her spring finals and summer semester, which wasn't much time, but anything to keep Ellen's focus off of Ryan, was welcomed.

When Ellen had returned from spring break, she had a meltdown in Katie's arms. Her friend lovingly listened to her whole story and soothingly calmed her troubled heart. Katie had been shocked at first and cautiously expressed her disappointment in not only Ellen's actions, but also the fact that she wouldn't allow the two of them to work it out.

"He obviously loves you Ellie. He proposed to you! Why are you rejecting him like this?" Katie held Ellen out at arm's length and continued to question her choices. Ellen listened and responded as best she could, even though Katie wasn't willing to accept her final decision.

Katie had come around over the last few weeks and finally decided to accept Ellen's decision after she realized Ellen wouldn't change her mind.

"I may not understand why and I probably never will, but I'll respect your decision and I'll do my best to help you move on."

Ellen hugged Katie and thanked her, saying she needed her support more than anything.

Ellen shut her notebook and looked out the window. The sun was beginning to set over the campus and Katie had asked her to meet for dinner down in the cafeteria. She glanced at her watch and decided it was time to head down. Katie had asked her to meet at 6:30 and it was already a quarter after.

She grabbed her sneakers and slipped them on, pulling the cuff of her jeans down over them. She pulled her knotty hair into a loose ponytail to get it out of her face and grabbed the key to their dorm room off of the little wooden table by the door.

The air was warm and inviting as she made her way across campus. Students were mingling together in front of the other dorms as she passed them and a late pick-up soccer game was happening in the open green space to her left. It was soothing to hear the cheering and chatting between students. It reminded Ellen that life continued, even after hardships. It gave her a quiet confidence to move forward and she knew good things would happen for her.

She pulled open the large glass door to the cafeteria and the pleasant aroma of fresh pizza hit her nose. Perfect! Just what she was in the mood for. She walked to the front and grabbed a slice of pepperoni and a slice of sausage. She filled a glass with ice-cold water and found a seat in a booth looking over the field, where the soccer game was finishing up.

There was no sign of Katie yet, which was typical. She was never one to be on time. "Fashionably late is always great," she would say. Ellen bit into her pizza as she waited for her friend and enjoyed the gooey goodness of the hot cheese on her tongue. She watched the remaining light from the sun fade to darkness and the lights around campus turn on. The cafeteria wasn't too full at the moment and the quietness gave Ellen some time to reflect on her future plans. She had things lined up, but she always wanted to be prepared for anything and everything. Ryan would always tell her that God had an ultimate plan and everything would always work out, without us having to worry about every little thing. Ellen liked having control of her own life though, and she would just smile and nod when Ryan would talk like that.

Katie sat down in the booth across from Ellen a few minutes later trying to suppress a huge grin on her face. "What's so funny?" Ellen asked.

"It's nothing funny. It's something exciting." Katie pulled a newspaper page from behind her back. "Look who made the front page!"

Ellen read the top part of the article, "LOCAL ATHLETE SHINES AT SPRING MINI-TRAINING CAMP." Below that was a picture of Ryan on the field with a bunch of other football players. He was wearing white shorts and a red training jersey and held a San Diego helmet by the facemask in his hands.

"I know you're trying to move on and whatnot, but I couldn't help myself. I had to show you this." Katie couldn't sit still in her seat, "I'm just so proud of him."

"I am too," Ellen replied. She took the page from Katie and read the article. It didn't say anything more that Ellen already knew. She glanced at his picture one more time and handed the newspaper back to Katie.

Katie folded it up and placed it on the seat next to her. "I'm going to grab some pizza. I'll be right back." Katie got up, her long, blond ponytail swishing behind her.

Ellen sighed again as she took another bite of her pizza. Getting over Ryan was going to be one of the most difficult things she would ever have to do.

CHAPTER TWENTY-THREE

Ryan was adjusting to the San Diego life. He was still in shock that he was on an NFL roster, something he had been dreaming about since he was a little boy. Now his dream was his reality and it was surreal. He took each day one by one, because things had been coming at him at a hundred miles an hour. His agent, Michael, had told him to just breathe and take things one step at a time. Michael informed Ryan that he would eventually get used to all the media attention, the demanding schedule and the lack of personal time. Ryan wasn't sure he would ever get used to it, but more than likely would just adapt to it and embrace it as his new lifestyle.

The head coach of San Diego, Martin, was a real down-to-earth coach. He was well liked by all the players and his quiet disposition put Ryan at ease. He felt as if his coach really took an interest when Ryan was speaking and it made the whole move to San Diego a much smoother transition.

Before Ryan had made the trip out here, he felt some reservations about it. Yes, he signed a contract and was obligated to go and he wasn't trying to get out of the move, but with everything that had gone on with Ellen, he didn't feel that moving across the country was the right thing to do. However, God had other plans and here he was in sunny California, living out his dream.

Ryan was used to being in the spotlight during his college career and the interest he had drummed up in the professional football world had continued to follow him. He wasn't a starter, but being a top draft pick made him a target for the media. He was slowly getting used to the heightened attention, but it was still a learning process for him. He was thankful for Michael's assistance in the process, because without him Ryan would be a floundering fish in and endless sea of paparazzi.

Ryan sat in his shared apartment with two other rookie draft picks, as they went over the revised playbook Coach had handed them that day. Antwon, a rookie wide receiver and Blake, a fifth round tight end, were his roommates. So far, the three of them had gotten along great and they had good chemistry on the field.

Antwon, drafted in the third round from the University of Pittsburgh, was most likely going to see a starting role in San Diego's offense. His speed and agility brought a quickness that San Diego needed on their team.

Blake, drafted out of OSU, was on the team in a back-up roll. He hoped to prove his worth on the team and then hopefully move up on the roster.

Ryan was the second string quarterback behind starter Darius Smith, but there was a possibility of taking Darius' spot on the roster if he could prove himself in training and during preseason. He would feel bad if he ousted Darius, but this was his job now, his career, and he needed to work hard at it.

Ryan focused on the playbook to the best of his ability,

taking note of the more complicated defensive fronts the NFL had to offer. All the veteran players talked about how big a difference there was between college football and professional and Ryan was slowly starting to realize it. Ryan made sure he was in constant communication with his teammates and his coaches. He needed to stay alert and up to date with everything to keep himself playing confidently.

Most of the drills that they had gone through so far in spring training camp were routine for Ryan, but he continued to take things as they came.

Ryan headed back into his room to get a little rest and time to himself before the evening activities started. The rookies and new players San Diego had picked up were going to go through some game film from last year to take note of the roles they would be stepping into.

Ryan had another urge to call Ellen, but he refrained, which he had been doing a lot lately. She never picked up anymore when he called. She never called back when he left voicemail messages either. He knew she was trying to keep her distance and move on, but Ryan missed her and wished more than anything she would be willing to work through this.

Yes, he was hurt by what she did, but she was human and humans make mistakes. He was sure people thought he was crazy for wanting her back, but he didn't care what other people thought. He hadn't talked to anyone other than his parents anyway and they were supportive of whatever he decided. They both had voiced they were disappointed in Ellen's actions, but they wouldn't stop loving her.

Ryan glanced at his phone one more time, but didn't pick it up. It was time to focus on his career now and put

Ellen in the past. He would try to keep his promise to her dad, but right now, without her responding, it was hard to do.

He closed his eyes, thankful for the peace and quiet right now from the chaotic world.

The next few weeks went well and Ryan was adjusting to his new way of life. He was learning the playbook and preparing himself for training camp in July. Right now, his life was filled with media sessions, interviews, endorsements and just trying to get to know his teammates and building chemistry with them.

He was planning a trip back home to visit his parents and a few of his friends from college tomorrow for two weeks. He wanted some time away to get his mind focused and ready for the next step in his career. Training camp was going to be tough and preseason was going to be even tougher, but he was determined.

He finished packing his suitcase and making travel arrangements to the airport in the morning. Antwon and Blake were in the living room playing Madden.

"Dude, you wanna join us?" Antwon pointed at the television screen and gestured at the open chair.

"Sure," Ryan said as he grabbed a controller and sat down.

For the next two hours, the three rookies enjoyed some competitive gameplay and laughter. Ryan was thankful for these two guys that God placed in his life as roommates. When training camp started up in July, coach had informed everyone that players would be rooming with different teammates, so Ryan was going to miss these guys. Rooming with another teammate would be beneficial though, because it helped the team to gel better.

Ryan put the controller down in surrender after Blake

scored a game winning touchdown. "You got me this time bro, but next time you won't see what's coming."

"We'll see about that. I think you're all talk," Blake countered.

"Guys, now we all know who the real talent in the group is," Antwon piped in as he stood up and puffed out his chest.

Ryan let the two of them argue amongst themselves about who was the better gamer and grabbed a bottle of water from the fridge.

He walked back to his room and grabbed his Bible that was sitting on top of his suitcase. He leafed through a few pages until he came to the passage in Proverbs he had been reading through. He read a few passages until his eyes became too heavy and he drifted off to sleep. Tomorrow he would head home to spend some time with his parents and God-willing maybe get to see Ellen as well.

CHAPTER TWENTY-FOUR

The plane ride was smooth and uneventful. Ryan made his way to the baggage claim to pick up his suitcase and kept a lookout for his parents. He was excited to see them and also ready to be back home and enjoy some downtime.

He rounded the corner after picking up his bag and spotted his mom and dad near the glass doors leading out to the bus lanes.

His mom squealed and ran to greet him, while his dad casually strolled up to him and gave him a hug.

"I've missed you guys!" Ryan exclaimed.

"We've missed you too, son." His dad patted him on the back and reached for his suitcase. "Let me get that for you."

Ryan let his dad handle his bag and thanked him.

"How was your plane ride?" his mom asked.

Ryan held the glass door open for his parents as they all made their way to the parking garage. "It was good. I'm just glad to be home right now."

Ryan's mom hugged him again and started filling him in on all that had been going on over the past two months.

Ryan smiled as his mom went on and on about things he

didn't have much of an interest in. "Ms. Sally down the street adopted another cat. I think she's up to eight now. It's the cutest little thing. Also, Mr. Grooms' fence is in disarray and I suggested that you could come over to help him fix it while you're home. I hope you don't mind."

"Sure mom, that's fine." Ryan didn't really want to work on a fence while he was on such a short break, but Mr. Grooms was an elderly man, across the street from his parents, and he shouldn't be tackling a project like that on his own. Ryan did enjoy listening to Mr. Grooms' war stories when he used to go over there during past summers. They would sit on his porch and sip lemonade while Roger, Mr. Grooms' first name, would reminisce about his younger days. Ryan continued to listen to his mom as she went on with her stories and looked forward to getting to talk to Roger, even though he wasn't too keen on helping repair a fence.

"June, why don't you let the boy talk a little about what's been going on with him. I don't think he's that interested in what your friends have been up to."

"Oh, I'm sorry sweetie," June turned to look at her son. "I was just so happy to have you home that I couldn't stop talking. Go on and tell us all about your life the past two months."

"It's ok mom, you can keep talking if you'd like. I'm just enjoying being home with you guys."

"No, go ahead. I've talked enough. I know your father wants to hear all about what's going on in the football world." She turned to her husband Rick and winked.

Ryan dove into a few of his many stories that had accumulated over the past two months. Sharing about his triumphs and even his struggles. His parents offered their encouragement and their support. Ryan was grateful.

"What is San Diego like?" his dad asked as he turned off the highway.

"It's pretty laid back, just like it is here. Sunny all the time and warm. I'm thankful a cold weather team didn't draft me. I'm not sure I could handle the lack of sun and freezing temperatures." Ryan and his parents all chuckled.

"Is Cameron going to be visiting while I'm home?" Ryan asked. Cameron was Ryan's older brother. He lived in Chicago with his wife Charlotte, where the two of them owned their own pizza restaurant.

"He said he'd be down by the end of the week for a few days. Unfortunately, Charlotte can't come down with him because they haven't been able to hire a new manager yet. She has to stay there to keep the restaurant running smoothly." Ryan's mom answered.

Ryan was bummed his sister-in-law wouldn't be able to visit, but he was thankful his brother was able to make the trip. He needed some bonding time with his brother and was hoping to have some one-on-one time to get advice on what to do about Ellen.

A few minutes later, his dad pulled into the driveway of Ryan's childhood home. He pushed open the car door and inhaled a deep breath of the fresh, South Carolina air. He grabbed his suitcase from the trunk and walked in the front door. Even though he hadn't been gone for that long, it felt like it had been ages since he set foot in this house. Soon his life would be even crazier and trips home like this wouldn't be nearly as frequent.

Ryan walked down the hallway to his bedroom towards the back of the house and stretched out on his bed. He pulled his phone from his pocket and remembered he had forgotten to turn it off of airplane mode. He switched it off and watched as a few messages popped up on his screen.

One from his parents saying they were at the airport and patiently waiting for him and another one from his buddy Cliff saying a few of the guys were getting together at Ripley's Sea House and wanted to see him. Ryan pulled up the reply screen and sent a quick message to Cliff.

Let me know when and I'll make sure to be there. Can't wait to see you guys.

He skimmed through the other messages, responding to the ones he needed to and set his phone down on his nightstand. The anticipation of coming home had drained him, so he closed his eyes and let sleep take over for a little bit.

He met the guys later that evening and filled them on everything that had been going on with him. It was a group of six of them, including his college roommate, Alex. They all sat around one of the round tables in the back of the restaurant. The walls were decorated with old fishing gear and photos of the owners from years ago. Ryan was thankful for the privacy, because even in this small town people knew who he was and wanted to talk to him.

The guys sat around listening to Ryan's stories and asking him all sorts of questions. The primary question brought up was if he had met any girls while he was out there. Ryan just calmly explained that he wasn't looking for anyone and needed to focus primarily on football. They all knew he and Ellen had broken up, but he didn't want to go into detail about it. They would never understand his willingness to continue pursuing her and would probably do their best to talk him out of it.

Cliff thankfully changed the subject for him and asked what was coming up next for him when he went back to San Diego. Ryan talked about training camp starting at the end of the month and what he was expecting going into the preseason. He talked about his battle to become the starting quarterback and all the guys chimed in saying they thought he would win that battle easily. Little did they know that the NFL was a lot tougher than college, but Ryan was appreciative of their confidence in him.

Another round of sodas and fried shrimp came to their table, as the guys began to reminisce. Ryan had grown up with these guys, attending elementary school, high school and doing life together. It felt good to dive back into a sense of nostalgia and be normal for the time being.

A few hours later Ryan had to call it a night and head back home. He promised the guys they would get together again before he left to head back. They all exchanged goodbyes and drove off in their various vehicles.

Ryan slipped behind the wheel of his mom's car, since his Jeep was in San Diego. A small urge to drive to the college campus to see Ellen crept up on him, but it was two hours away and it would be too late in the night to see her. Instead, he grabbed his phone from his pocket and decided to call her before he headed back home. He didn't think she'd answer, but he was willing to give it a try, at least to let her know that he was home for the next two weeks.

It rang four times and went straight to voicemail, but Ryan didn't leave a message. He decided he would carve out some time to drive up there and surprise her. He knew she was taking summer classes to graduate a year early and usually there weren't many students around campus this time of the year, so he figured she would be easy to find.

He started his mom's car and pulled out of the parking lot. He drove home in silence, sending up a few prayers just asking God to allow Ellen to be willing to listen to him.

CHAPTER TWENTY-FIVE

This summer semester was proving itself pretty difficult for Ellen, but she enjoyed the challenge. It was propelling her closer to her dream and that's what she focused on. Her classes were stimulating, which kept her going, despite how difficult they were. Diving into the sciences of different sports was intriguing her as well. Football was still the primary sport she was interested in, but she found herself allowing the possibilities of other sports' avenues to invade her thoughts.

With Katie home for the summer, Ellen had moved into a much smaller dorm room on the other side of campus. She lived by herself, which was nice because it gave her plenty of time for her studies. She had made a new friend through this whole process, Johanna, and the two girls usually studied together, pressing each other with the difficult questions.

Johanna was a quiet girl, very studious, which meshed well with Ellen's personality. When they got together, they both remained focused, unlike the few times Ellen had tried to study with Katie. She loved Katie to death, but the girl did not make a very good study partner.

Johanna would be graduating after the summer courses and was planning on moving back out to California, where most of her family lived. She was one of many students tracking Ryan in his NFL career and hoped to write many articles about him when she returned to California. Her love was basketball though and with her tall, athletic build, she was great on the court as well. Her dark skin and wild curly hair were very striking and her dark green eyes gave her an exotic flair that had the guys lining up. Johanna's shy nature kept them at bay and Ellen was thankful for a friend that wasn't focused on relationships right now. It helped her as she continued to move on without a relationship of her own.

Ellen had heard Ryan was back in town for a week or so before training camp and the football season started. A part of her wanted to see him, but she knew better and Johanna was good at reminding her that it wouldn't help her as she moved forward with her life and career goals.

Ellen looked down at her notes and went over them one more time before turning out her desk light. There was a big presentation that was due tomorrow and her nerves were starting to take over. She didn't let them get to her though, because she was prepared and ready to go. She felt good about it and knew that she'd make her professor proud.

Ellen shut her notebook and slid it into her backpack. She put on her silky pajama bottoms and matching tank top, then switched off the light. As darkness overcame the room, Ellen rehearsed her speech one more time in her head and eventually fell asleep. She was one step closer to accomplishing her dream and that was something to be happy about.

~*~

Cameron was finally in town and Ryan was thrilled. He needed some time with his older brother and he was thankful for this opportunity before life became more hectic for him.

Cameron had his dark hair cut short and his blue eyes still sparkled with enthusiasm. They definitely didn't resemble each other, looking more like good friends rather than brothers, but the brotherly bond they shared ran deep. A few wrinkles invaded the corner of Cameron's eyes, which Ryan figured was the onset of the stress from running his own business.

Cameron talked about the restaurant and how Charlotte was doing. She had expressed how sorry she was that she wasn't able to make it down, but hoped to come the next time.

The family spent the next few hours catching up on life and Cameron congratulated his little brother on finding success with his dream. He asked him the same questions his parents had asked, but Ryan didn't mind repeating his answers. It felt good to talk about his dream becoming a reality for him.

A little later Ryan asked Cameron to come sit out on the back deck with him. "I have some things I want to run by you and get your advice on."

"Sure thing bro." Cameron grabbed a bottle of water from the fridge and handed one to Ryan as they made their way outside to the back patio.

The sun began to set, cooling the air a few degrees to make it tolerable, more so than it had been earlier in the day.

"So, what is it you have on your mind?" Cameron took a sip of his water and turned to Ryan, waiting for his answer.

"It's about Ellie." Ryan launched into the whole story and explained the feelings he had been struggling with.

"I love her and I don't think I can ever stop loving her, but she won't talk to me anymore. I know it's because she needs her space, but I just don't know what to do and I'm very confused."

Cameron nodded after his brother finished his story and paused a second before answering. "Have you prayed about it?"

Ryan nodded, "I have, but I don't seem to be getting any answers. At least nothing that I can decipher and see clearly."

"Well, I think that answer is pretty clear, bro. You even said she needs her space and I think that's your answer. You both need space and time apart."

"I know that, but for how long? Should I stop trying to talk to her altogether or still communicate with her just to let her know I still care; to let her know I still want her in my life?" Ryan downed the rest of his water and tossed his empty water bottle in the nearby recycling bin. He leaned forward, folding his hands on his knees.

"You need to stop altogether. I know that sounds impossible right now, but you need to focus on God first and then your new career second. Cut Ellen out right now. God says, 'All things work together for the good of those who love Him,' even if that means letting go of someone we love. There was a time when Charlotte and I were separated shortly after we were engaged and I thought I was going to lose her, but it turns out God was just trying to get us to set our priorities straight. I had lost complete focus on Him and was focusing solely on Charlotte. That time apart helped both of us fix our eyes on Him first and it has helped our relationship tremendously. At the time, we both thought it was a cruel ending, but it turns out, it was all for the best. So, I think you need to let Ellen go, as hard as that might sound, and move on for now. If it's meant to be, God will bring her back into your life, but for now you need to follow Him alone." Cameron patted Ryan on the shoulder, "I'll be praying for you."

Ryan sighed, a part of him knew this is how the conversation with his brother was going to go, but it was hard hearing it and Ryan did not feel prepared to deal with all of this. His brother was right though and he needed to get his priorities straight, no matter how difficult it was going to be.

He thanked his brother and they exchanged a hug. "If you ever need to talk or even vent a little, I'm here for you."

Ryan nodded and thanked his brother again.

The rest of the evening, Ryan enjoyed his time with family and felt grateful for the blessing of these people in his life. That night while he lay in bed staring up at the ceiling, he reached and grabbed his phone off of his nightstand. He found Ellen's number and hovered over the delete button. "God I pray that she finds you in this time apart. Keep her safe and allow her to achieve her dreams. I think she deserves it. Thank you for the time we had together and if it's Your will, please bring her back to me someday."

He pressed delete at that moment and erased the girl he loved from his phone, but not from his heart. As difficult as this moment was for him, he knew it was right. A comforting peace washed over him as he drifted off to sleep, ready to begin this next phase of his life.

CHAPTER TWENTY-SIX

The warm, southern breeze pushed her dark brown curls away from her face as she focused on the sky. The clouds tried to suffocate the sun, but the sun pushed back, casting its rays down onto the ocean. It gave the waves a gentle sparkle as they waltzed their way to the shore. It was angelic in a way, as if he was present here with her.

She pulled her knees to her chest and wrapped her arms around them, inhaling a deep breath of warm, salty air. It had been just over a year now, a year filled with regret and a longing that had never left her heart. A year from the day she let go of the best thing that had ever happened to her. It was the hardest thing she had ever done and she still had to convince herself that it was the best thing. The right thing to do. Ryan needed a girl that was faithful, trustworthy and that shared in his faith. She was none of those things. She reminded herself of those facts every day.

"Eric, I know in my head what I did was right for Ryan and for myself, but why does my heart not feel that way too?" She turned and looked at the cross, tucked away in the middle of the dunes. It had been four years since that horrible accident and not a moment passed by that she didn't miss her best friend. She wished he were here to help her through the mess she had caused.

She closed her eyes and let the sound of the ocean waves speak to her, hopeful that something would be decipherable, but there was nothing.

"I thought this would be a lot easier to deal with now that we've gone our separate ways and are living our different lives. Unfortunately, it's not." Ellen took in a shaky breath, gaining control of her emotions.

She strolled over, kneeled down and placed her hand on Eric's cross, drawing strength from it as if her best friend was sitting right next to her. A warm breeze swirled around her and she knew it was Eric. She knew he was saying that no matter what he was always still there with her. It gave her a renewed energy as she stood up, brushed the sand off of her shorts and began walking towards the parking lot.

She carried her flip-flops in her hand, as she let her feet sink into the soft sand, leaving footprints behind her. She turned and glanced at Eric's cross one more time before advancing any further. She blew a kiss in its direction and continued walking forward.

Her spring semester was soon over and she would be graduating in three weeks. Ellen couldn't believe how the time had passed and that she would be moving on in this world, accomplishing her dreams. She already had a full-time job lined up in Charlotte, North Carolina where she would be writing online sports articles for a local news company. She had written some pieces for them before and they were eager to have her come on board with them. Ellen was thankful for the opportunity and glad she was already set up in the working world to start her new journey. It wasn't going to be high paying or anything that would reach millions of readers around the world, but it was a start and Ellen was going to make the most of it. This would be the first step into the new adventure of her life and Ellen was excited.

She pulled into her parents' driveway and opened the front door to the smell of something delicious being concocted in the kitchen.

"Smells delightful, Mom!" she exclaimed as she made her way back to her childhood bedroom to do a little studying before dinner. Finals started in a little over a week and Ellen had come home for the weekend to spend some time with her parents, before finals started. It also gave her some quiet time to study.

Her emotions started to get to her as she realized how soon she was going to be leaving college to go out into the real world. Farther from her parents and farther from Katie, who still had a year of college left to go. Katie planned to visit Ellen as often as she could once Ellen found an apartment in Charlotte. Ellen had some leads on a few places already and next weekend she was going up with her parents to check them out. Everything just felt so surreal, like she wasn't old enough yet to be going out and doing these things, but here she was.

Ellen pulled out her notebooks and began going over her notes, waiting for her mom's announcement that dinner was ready.

At the dinner table, Ellen's parents went over the plans for the following weekend and made sure everything was ready to go. They went over the potential prospects that Ellen had lined up and the places they thought would be the best.

"I heard Ryan was made the official starter for San Diego this upcoming season," Ellen's dad blurted out.

"Colt!" Meredith glared at her husband. They had tried their best not to mention Ryan around Ellen, knowing that it was a sore subject for their daughter.

"It's okay Mom. I don't mind. I actually read about it online this morning, so I already knew." Ellen put a spoonful of mashed potatoes in her mouth as she glanced up at both of her parents. "Seriously, I'm fine now. We don't have to avoid the subject anymore." She knew what she said wasn't completely true, but she knew her dad followed Ryan's career.

Her dad went on to talk about what he had read in the article and Ellen politely listened to him. She also tried to ignore the fact that her dad was beaming uncontrollably. Her dad cared deeply about Ryan and it made Ellen feel guilty about everything all over again. She tried not to focus on it.

Ryan's first year in the NFL had gone pretty smoothly, if you considered all that had happened. In his third preseason game, he went down with a broken collarbone that sidelined him for eight weeks. He was gunning to become the starter, but after the injury, quarterback Darius Smith got his starting job back. Ryan had been devastated as he stated in multiple interviews that Ellen had watched. It didn't help with the 'getting over him' process, but Ellen couldn't help it. She wanted to know how he was doing and the fact that he was top news around the country made it hard not to see and hear things.

After his eight weeks of healing were up, Ryan spent time on the bench watching Darius live out his dream. Every once in a while, Ryan would step onto the field for a special gadget play, but very rarely did those plays work out for him. With three games left in the season and a game behind the division leader, Darius went down with a broken ankle. Ryan was called to step in and Ellen watched every second of those last three games. A local restaurant aired the San Diego games in support of their homegrown football star and Ellen was there every Sunday to watch him play.

Ryan came out onto the field in that first game with ease, as if he had been playing in the NFL his whole life. The other two games he looked just as good, leading San Diego to its first division title in eleven years. Ellen was beaming when the seconds ticked off the clock in that final game, because San Diego was going to the playoffs and it was all because of Ryan.

Watching the postgame interview after that game was the most memorable moment of that entire day. Ellen remembered every word clearly.

Ronald, the interviewer, was asking Ryan a series of questions about the game and the season as a whole. He asked Ryan about his emotions and what his first year in the league felt like.

Ryan answered every question with poise and confidence, but the final question Ryan answered for Ron was what took up a permanent residence in her heart.

"Do you have a girl back home where you're from in South Carolina that's cheering you on right now? A lot of your female fans are hoping for a 'no' here, so choose your answer wisely." Ron winked at the camera.

Ryan folded his hands in his lap as he leaned forward in his chair. He looked right into the camera as he answered, his eyes intent on searching for that one viewer.

"Actually Ron, I do, but not in the way you're implying. At least not right now. I have a girl back home that I hold in my heart and always will, no matter where life takes us. Right now life has taken us down separate roads. Maybe

155

one day they will cross again and I hope and pray that's the outcome, but if not, then I know that the small portion of my life she was part of will be safely tucked in my heart forever."

Ellen swallowed the lump that had caught in her throat, but in that moment, Ryan was looking directly at her, as if hundreds and hundreds of miles were not separating them at all right now. She knew he meant it and it made her heart hurt all over again. She tried to watch the rest of the interview, but the tears blurred her vision and she couldn't bear to listen anymore.

Two weeks later, in the divisional round of the playoffs, Ryan tried his best to lead San Diego to a playoff win. Unfortunately, they lost in the end, 27-19.

Sitting at the table with her parents, listening to her dad go on about Ryan's statistics, she smiled. Yes, her heart ached to go back in time and fix her mistake, but mistakes were learning experiences in life and Ellen was learning from hers. She held on to the peace of knowing that both she and Ryan were setting out to accomplish their dreams and ultimately that's what both of them had wanted for each other. Ellen remained content in the fact.

CHAPTER TWENTY-SEVEN

Training camp and OTA's had been challenging and strengthening all at the same time. Ever since Ryan was named the starter for San Diego's upcoming season, he pushed himself even harder to be the best he could be. He would never forget the day his coach and San Diego's general manager, Al Roman, invited him into his coach's expansive office. They outlined what they expected of him during the season and then surprised him with the news of being the official starter. Ryan had thanked them profusely and promised them both that he wouldn't let them down.

The first preseason game of the season was coming up and Ryan was using most of his time to work with his guys to get the timing down for their routes. He wanted them to be able to run the offense with such precision that defenses would struggle all season to keep them under control. Antwon was becoming a real star after getting his first season under his belt and Blake, his tight end, was always reliable over the middle for large gains. Ryan was positive they were going to be strong contenders again this season.

Ryan's phone went off with a text from his agent letting him know that an article was posted online that he thought

Ryan would want to read. Ryan clicked on the link that Michael sent him and the page opened up on his phone.

The title, <u>WHEN FAITH KILLS YOUR IMAGE</u>, was the first thing that caught Ryan's eyes. Again, with the slams on his faith. During the offseason, Ryan had made it very clear where he stands in life and Who his primary focus was. The media loved to have a field day with it and tried in every way possible to make him look stupid for having such a public faith. It never hurt Ryan's feelings, because he knew who he was in Christ and he was called to be a living light in this world. He wasn't going to stop just because it was unorthodox when it came to the professional sports world.

Ryan took the time to read the article and afterwards felt pushed to make even more of a difference. There were hurting people in this world that needed an example like him in their life and that's what he had set out to do. He texted Michael back and thanked him for sending the link. Michael pushed Ryan to be verbal about his faith, because the positive image was good for publicity and jersey sales. Michael may not have the best reasoning behind it, but at least he was positive about Ryan sharing his faith.

Ryan also texted Michael to let him know that he was looking into some charities or even possibly starting his own. He was saving up a lot of money with his contract and all the endorsements he was receiving; now he needed to start making a difference with it.

Michael agreed with him, only because of the publicity, but at least he was willing to help Ryan with the process.

Ryan set his phone back down on his desk and went back to studying his playbook. He wanted to be sharp for the opening preseason game.

~*~

Ellen was enjoying her job and was starting to move up in the company after her articles had received rave reviews from her readers. Her boss was singing her praises lately and with football season approaching quickly, he had her on the lead for their online website. Ellen was ecstatic when Leonard, her boss, shared the news with her.

Ellen was busy typing away on her next piece. It was a story about a local soccer star that had made himself well known in Europe's league. Soccer wasn't her favorite sport, but she had grown to like it after getting to know Stefan and his love for the sport. He was Real Madrid's lead scorer and had made a name for himself during the World Cup over the summer. He had come home to visit with his family and Ellen had been asked to interview him.

After she had this story published, she would move into her new position and football would be her primary focus. Ellen was elated with the new aspirations she was making for herself.

A few minutes later Leonard approached her desk and gently tossed a magazine onto the corner of it. A page towards the middle was flipped open. "Looks like they enjoy smacking your boy around."

Ellen stopped what she was doing and looked at whatever Leonard was talking about. She saw the title and cringed. The media was slamming Ryan about his faith again. Leonard enjoyed bringing every article he could find about Ryan to Ellen's attention, because he was thrilled with the fact that Ellen had a former connection with the upcoming star. Ellen knew he expected her to write with the kind of caliber that most of the other top authors wrote with, but Ellen refused to attack someone because of their faith, especially Ryan.

"This will be you soon. Global recognition for your hard work and dedication." Leonard leaned against her desk and stared at her. "Are you ready to move forward Ellen?"

"Yes, I'm ready to move up in this company and I'm thankful that you are giving me this opportunity, but Leonard I don't feel comfortable writing like that. I could never attack someone personally like that."

"Well, sometimes you have to do what you have to do in the writing world to move up. If you want to move on to bigger companies someday you'll have to mix it up and throw in an edgy piece every once in a while. It's good for your career. Don't worry about it." Leonard chuckled as he walked away and began whistling a cheery tune.

Ellen leaned back in her chair and stared at the article. She hoped she would never have to write something like that, but that she could stick to what she knew and loved. She wanted to write about her passion for football and the positives coming from the sport. She hoped Leonard was wrong, but she understood what he was saying.

Ellen pushed her thoughts aside and focused on her current piece on Stefan. She wanted to finish this today and get it ready to publish on the website tomorrow. Preseason football started in a few days and she needed to get some material started for that. She looked around her small cubicle and realized this was her last article she would be writing in this cramped space. After this, she was moving upstairs to her own office. Ellen smiled, she got this far with her writing and she knew with her talent she could make it even farther. She pushed Leonard's comments from her mind and decided to prove him wrong instead.

That evening Ellen curled up with a good book in her downtown apartment. She had been invited to go out for a few drinks with her coworkers, but decided to spend a quiet evening at home instead. With her new promotion going into effect, she wanted to get herself mentally prepared and rested.

A knock sounded on the door and Ellen lifted her fuzzy, purple blanket off of her lap and ambled over to the door. She looked out the peephole to see who it was and was delighted to see Katie standing in the hallway.

Ellen threw open the door and hugged her friend. "I'm so glad to see you! What brings you to this neighborhood?"

Katie squeezed her friend in delight. "I wanted to come see you and congratulate you on your new promotion!"

"You came all the way to tell me that? I feel so honored!" Ellen giggled and turned to let her friend into the apartment.

"Well, I kind of met a guy and he's from this area too, so I'm also here for him. I came to see you first though." Katie laughed and plopped down on the couch.

"Oh, I see how it is. I'm glad I'm first on your list of things to see." Ellen sat down next to her friend and they both continued to talk as if no time had passed between them. The summer had been busy for the both of them and with Ellen moving to Charlotte, they hadn't had near as much time together as they had planned.

Katie's hands were flying as she was describing the new guy she had met and Ellen smiled, thankful that her friend was happy with someone. Ellen felt a bit of jealousy creep up, but she shoved it back down.

Katie went on saying she had met Adam on a retreat she had helped with over the summer. He had been in charge of the 4th grade boys' cabin, while she worked in the cafeteria and coordinated the afternoon games. They had really hit it off and continued to stay in contact afterwards and Katie continuously stated how she felt he was the one. "I know we've only known each other for a little over a month, but it's unlike anything I've ever felt before. It's the same way you said you felt about Ryan." Katie quickly covered her mouth with her hand and her blue eyes grew large. "Oh my gosh, Ellie, I am so sorry. I didn't mean to bring that up." Katie put her hand back in her lap.

"It's okay Katie, really. I'm so happy you found someone that makes you feel that way." Ellen reached over and grabbed Katie's hand, squeezing it to let her know it was okay.

Katie squeezed back and continued with her news. Ellen leaned back into the cushion of the couch and watched her animated friend. She was so thankful for this vibrant girlfriend. Katie brought spice into Ellen's life and she made things exciting, even with the distance separating them.

The two of them enjoyed the rest of the evening exchanging news and sipping strawberry wine. A new promotion, living out her dreams and a beautiful forever friend in her life... Ellen's heart was beyond content, for the most part.

CHAPTER TWENTY-EIGHT

It was that time of year again. Playoffs. Ryan was thrilled to be leading his team on the road to the Super Bowl for a second year in a row. After the heart-breaking loss in the Divisional Round last season, Ryan was glad to be getting a second shot at it. It had been a challenging season up to this point, with some injuries to key players, but everyone was healthy now and ready to begin their playoff journey.

Ryan was having a career year, but he couldn't have done it without his coaches backing him and his teammates rallying around him. There was talk about him winning MVP of the league, but he knew what he accomplished in the playoffs would be the deciding factor in that decision. Ryan couldn't help smiling at the thought of receiving that honor. It would truly be a dream come true, especially since this was only his second year in the league.

Ryan was currently second in the league in quarterback statistics, behind Drew Branson. If Ryan could dominate in the playoffs and add to his growing totals, he had a chance of edging Drew out for the prestigious award. Drew was the quarterback for Minnesota and they hadn't been able to secure a playoff spot. This was Ryan's chance and he would do everything he could to lead his team to victory and maybe even put his name on the MVP trophy.

Ryan sat in his cozy apartment sorting fan mail. He enjoyed taking the time to read what fans wrote to him and even respond to them when he could. Unfortunately, there wasn't enough time in his schedule to respond to all of them. His fan base was growing rapidly and he felt even more pressure to live as a light for them, especially the kids. He wanted them to know that no matter what you did in life you needed to embrace who you were and never let anyone try to change you. Lately, Ryan had been making many headlines with his openness about his faith. Most were good, but there was always one or two articles out there making fun of him or trying to tear him down. He never let it get to him or discourage him. He was doing exactly what God called him to do and that was all that mattered.

After scanning through all the fan mail, he turned his laptop on to skim through his email. The screen popped up and he clicked the login button to his email account. A few seconds later, all the unopened mail loaded and he started to go through them one by one. The few he knew were junk he instantly deleted and he saved the ones that pertained to his endorsements. He also saved the few that were reminders from his agent. One popped up about what was going to be discussed in the team meeting that evening and Ryan read that one to prepare himself.

As he scrolled down through a few more, he came upon an unfamiliar email address. The subject line read, Interview, so Ryan clicked on it, figuring it was just a random media person, as it usually was.

My boss has asked me to do a phone interview with you to run

a story before you guys jump into the playoff race. I'll be
contacting your agent with all the details and I hope to hear from
you soon. The interview won't take long… I know you have a
busy schedule. Thank you in advance,

Ellen Kane

It was his Ellie. His heart slammed against his chest and
he immediately got Michael on the phone to find out the
details about the interview.

"Hey Mike, I have an email here about a phone
interview I'm supposed to be doing. Do you know
anything about it?" His voice was shaky with the thought
of talking to Ellen again.

"Yes, Ellen Kane is her name. She will be calling you in
about an hour to do it. Is this the Ellen… you know… your
Ellen?"

Ryan sucked in a deep breath and slowly let out some air
before responding, "Yes, it's her."

"Well what a nice little reunion for you two. I hope it
goes well."

"Yeah, me too." Ryan touched the red button on his
phone, ending the conversation between him and Michael.
What in the world was he going to say to her? It had been
almost two years since they had talked last.

Ryan finished straightening up his desk and set the fan
mail he wanted to try to respond to in a drawer. Ryan
leaned back in his chair and stared at his phone. Was this
going to be the stepping-stone to get her back? He certainly
hoped so. There wasn't a day that went by where he didn't
think about her. His teammates thought he was nuts, but
he knew deep down that he couldn't let her go, at least not
yet.

Ryan did a few things around the small apartment,

straightening up the kitchen and putting things away. With the money he was making he planned to buy a large house in the suburbs of San Diego. His parents were planning to move out here to be closer to him, so he was hoping to buy a place large enough that they could move in with him. Once the offseason rolled around he would get all of those plans put into motion. For now, he was comfortable in his little downtown apartment.

His phone began to chime and he ran across his living room to grab it off of his desk. An unknown number flashed on the screen and he figured it had to be Ellen calling for the interview.

Ryan inhaled sharply and hit the call answer button. "Hello," he voiced.

"Hi Ryan, it's Ellen. Ready for your interview?"

"Ellie, it's so good to hear your voice. You have no idea."

He barely heard the quiet sigh on the other end of the line, but he heard it and that's what mattered. He knew with that one sound that she still cared and that is all he needed to hold onto the hope that still existed in the deepest part of his heart.

"It's good to hear your voice too, Ryan."

Before Ryan could say anything else, Ellen launched into her interview questions. Ryan became entranced by the sound of her voice and provided the best answers he could.

"What are your emotions like going into the playoffs?"

"Well, I'm nervous. Can't lie about that, but I'm more excited than nervous. Excited to see the team succeed and hopefully have a shot at going to the Super Bowl. I pray every night that God's will be done, but I secretly hope that's a Super Bowl championship for us."

"That would certainly be an incredible accomplishment for the city of San Diego. They have been in a Super Bowl drought now for over thirty years. Do you feel pressure knowing that history?"

"I feel pressure in every game. The coaches, my teammates and the San Diego fans all want that Lombardi Trophy brought home to San Diego. All I can do though is play my best."

He heard her shuffling some papers around and wanted to say something to her. He so badly wanted to tell her that he still loved her, but he didn't want to distract her from her job. He hoped she would be able to chat a little bit after the interview. He had some time before the team meeting that evening.

"Okay, one final question before we're finished here. What makes you tick Ryan? What makes you the player you are on and off the field?"

"That's actually two questions," Ryan chuckled, but didn't hear a response from Ellen. He could picture her smiling though.

"I'd have to say first and foremost that God is behind everything I do. He's the one that gave me the abilities that I have and He's the one that gives me the opportunity to do what I do day in and day out. But there's one other thing that drives me."

Ryan heard more pages flipping, "What's that?" Ellen asked.

"You Ellie, you drive me."

~*~

Two days later Ellen submitted her article from the phone interview with Ryan. He had answered her questions perfectly and she was really satisfied with her finished piece. She dropped the paper off in Leonard's office and headed out to the parking lot. Tomorrow was her last day working for the Charlotte Online Tribune. A job offer from New York had come her way and she had no choice but to accept such an incredible opportunity. She would be writing for one of the top sports' magazines in the country, Magnitude.

She had been contacted by a guy named Jim Lorenzo about a month ago stating he had been reading her articles for the past two months and was awed by her writing talent. He praised her on each and every piece he had read so far and said he needed someone like her on his team in New York.

Ellen had been beyond thrilled with the invitation, but told Jim she wanted to think it over before she made a final decision. He said he completely understood and hoped she would say yes.

She went to her parents' beach cottage that weekend and talked with them about the new job offer. They both were thrilled for her and even though they would both miss her dearly, they knew she couldn't pass up such a significant opportunity. Even Katie was bubbling with enthusiasm at the thought of Ellen going to New York City.

Ellen had called Jim the following Monday and let him know that yes, she would be glad to join the Magnitude magazine team.

The past two weeks had been filled with travel to New York to find a place to live and to visit the facilities of her new job. Her heart would not slow down with all of the excitement coming her way. This was actually happening for her.

She was sad to be leaving Leonard and her other

coworkers, but she was moving on to bigger and better things and she was ready. This is what she had always dreamed of doing.

Leonard wanted her last piece to be stellar before she left and that's why he had asked her to do the phone interview with Ryan Salas. At first, Ellen had been very reluctant, not wanting to bring up old emotions, but afterwards she felt lighthearted and content. She was thankful for the opportunity to talk to him, even though it was only on a professional level. She had sensed that Ryan wanted to talk more, but she ended the conversation as soon as the interview was over. She did not want to play with his feelings and she knew she certainly couldn't go through the process of trying to let him go again. His last comment still resonated deep in her soul, but she tried not to let it consume her. They were in completely different worlds now and the past was the past. There was nothing Ellen could do to go back and fix the wrong she had done and no matter how much her heart missed Ryan, she knew he needed someone better.

The wind whipped at her jacket as she made her way to her car. The air had a slight chill to it, but that was expected with January weather. Ellen opened her car door and sat down. She started the engine and waited for the heat to kick on. She leaned back in her seat and closed her eyes, taking in a deep breath. This was it... on to New York she would go.

CHAPTER TWENTY-NINE

New York living was a dream so far. Sure, she missed her calm, beachside life, but the hustle and bustle of New York was an exciting experience for Ellen. She curled up with some of her notes on her black, leather loveseat in her cozy, studio apartment. It had an exposed brick wall, with a bay window, in her living room and dining room combination. The kitchen was a mix of modern and old world charm, same as her two bathrooms. It was different and that's why Ellen decided to rent it as soon as she set her eyes on it.

She had been in New York for a little over a month now and there was still so much to do and see. She was adjusting to her new job and was beginning to love the atmosphere of the big magazine company. Magnitude was a magazine Ellen had seen her dad reading over the years. To be writing for them was a dream come true.

She flipped through her notes, preparing to work alongside Eli, her easy-going coworker. Eli was laid back and quiet, always contemplating and completely focused on his work. Ellen enjoyed his company and was thankful that Eli had offered to take her 'under his wing,' as he had put it. His wild, curly hair was a stark contrast to his calm personality. He was the biggest reason Ellen had adjusted so well to life in New York

Ellen's boss, Jim Lorenzo, had asked them to work on an article together for the Super Bowl and Ellen was thankful for the opportunity. Eli was moving to Texas within the next month for another job prospect and Ellen was really hoping that she would be able to take Eli's spot with the magazine. She had hinted to Jim about her interest.

The past week they had been collaborating together and tonight Ellen was gathering what she had and putting it into a structured article. Eli and she would combine their final thoughts tomorrow. Ellen was satisfied with what she had and decided that to put any more thought into it would cause her to change things that were better off left as they were.

She set her paper on the glass coffee table and went into her cute, compact kitchen to fix something for dinner. As she was heating up some leftover lasagna, she heard a knock at her apartment door.

She walked across her living room to the door and peered through the peephole to see who it was. A guy stood there holding a beautiful bouquet of flowers.

Ellen opened the door. "Hi."

"Hello, I'm looking for an Ellen Kane," the young man asked.

"Yes, I'm her."

"Well then, these are for you." He handed her the bouquet and a little pad to sign.

Ellen scribbled her signature quick and turned back into her apartment. She took a whiff of the flowers and let the sweet aroma tickle her nose. She peeked around for a card to see who they were from and saw it tucked into the side.

She reached for it and opened it up.

Thank you for the last few weeks. I have enjoyed working with you and getting to know you. I will certainly miss you when I leave for Texas.

Sincerely, Eli.

Ellen smiled at the note. She too had enjoyed getting to know Eli over the past few weeks and hoped they would be able to stay in touch as friends after he left.

Ellen grabbed a ceramic vase from her storage chest in her bedroom and filled it with water. She placed the sweet scented flowers in the vase and set them on her coffee table, so she could admire them.

She walked back into her kitchen to retrieve her lasagna and curled up in the living room to watch some television. She had been on an HGTV kick lately, getting ideas on how to decorate her apartment and dreaming one day of owning a large home that she could also decorate.

Work the next day went smoothly as her and Eli settled on their final format for their joint piece for Magnitude. It was a good breakdown of the upcoming, head-to-head matchup between Miami and Washington.

Ellen had been disappointed for Ryan this season. San Diego had been leading Miami the entire time during their championship matchup, but in the final two minutes of the fourth quarter, Miami rallied against San Diego's defense to score the winning touchdown, sealing their trip to the Super Bowl.

Ellen had watched the post-game interview later that night and the disappointment on Ryan's face caused an ache in Ellen's chest. She had known how badly he wanted to go to the Super Bowl. He had won MVP of the league, which she was proud of him for, but it's not the same as a Super Bowl ring and she knew he felt the same.

Yes, it stung. He had wanted that win more than anything, but he was young and he knew he had plenty of chances to get to the Super Bowl. He had been honored the night his name was called for MVP and the trophy shined in his case he had against a wall in his living room. He took pride in it. Being named MVP was a huge accomplishment, especially because this had been only his second year in the league. He still wanted that Super Bowl ring though and he was determined to get it someday.

He sat on his living room couch going over available homes along the coast. His parents were officially moving out here to be with him and he wanted to find a home where they could have their own space. There was a spacious villa, with a private guesthouse that was intriguing to him and he put in a call to his realtor to schedule a showing. His parents would be flying in tomorrow morning, so they would be able to go along with him and check the place out.

He shut his laptop, exhausted from the endless searching. He placed it on his desk and plugged it in. He sorted through his mail that had gathered into a large pile on the corner of the coffee table. He shredded the junk and towards the bottom came across an issue of Magnitude. He always enjoyed reading this magazine; he had been reading it since he was a little kid. He sat back down on the couch and started leafing through the glossy pages. The issue was over a month old, but that didn't deter him from reading the articles. He stopped on a page with an article about the matchup for the Super Bowl and began to read. He wanted to see the writer's perspective on the two teams, especially since Ryan knew Washington had dominated Miami. The writer was completely unbiased between the two teams, which made the article worth reading. It was interesting to read how in depth they had gotten with each teams' strengths and weaknesses. Ryan got to the end of the article and glanced down to see who wrote the article. It was a collaboration piece between a guy named Eli White and a girl, Ellen Kane.

Ryan smiled. Seeing her name in such a prominent magazine was exciting. Knowing that her dreams were coming true gave Ryan a calmness in his soul. She had to be happy and he was thankful for that, because she deserved it.

~*~

TWO YEARS LATER

The energy was electric and Ellen was beyond thrilled to be present here tonight. Now that she was one of the top writers for Magnitude, Jim had sent her to the site of the Super Bowl. She had always dreamed of going to the biggest game in the country, but she didn't think that dream would ever come true.

San Diego had finally made it after being excluded from the playoffs the season before. Ryan had gone down with a devastating ACL tear, but had bounced back this season with a renewed energy that no one had expected. Ellen was honored to be witnessing this historical moment in his career.

She had a seat in the press box, giving her an unobstructed view of the entire field. It was unlike any football game she had ever been to before. The singing of the national anthem had concluded and kick-off was coming up. Ellen took her seat, even though the adrenaline level she was experiencing made it hard to sit still.

The coin toss commenced and San Diego won it. They opted to defer and prepared to send their defense out onto the field.

The first half started slowly, each team putting a field goal on the board. Ryan was having a hard time getting his passes off. His offensive line was struggling against Green Bay's defense. They had a minute and half before halftime and Ryan was finally able to get into a rhythm, leading his team down the field and running in for a two-yard touchdown. It put them up 10-3. His teammates chest bumped and slapped his helmet after his daring run into the end zone.

The band for the halftime show put on a good concert, but Ellen was ready to get back to the game. Her nerves were all sorts of twisted and she so badly wanted San Diego to pull this off. Seeing Ryan hoist that Lombardi trophy would be the highlight of her writing career.

The teams came out of their respective locker rooms and Ellen's palms began to sweat. If she couldn't handle this pressure, how was Ryan?

She took a few deep breaths and watched as Ryan led the offense back out onto the field to start the second half. Once again, Ryan was being hit from all sides and his offensive line didn't seem to have an answer for any of Green Bay's defensive lineups.

They walked back to their bench as their punter kicked the ball back to Green Bay. That's when Ellen saw Ryan get down on his knees on the sideline with his offense and start praying. She didn't have to be down there to know what he was doing, she knew. It was one of the things she had always admired about him. Throughout his whole career, he had made his faith his identity and no matter how much the media tried to tear him apart; he kept strong. Ellen snapped a picture of them and planned to use it in her article.

The defense stayed strong and held Green Bay to another field goal, making the score 10-6. San Diego's offense ran back onto the field and Ryan pointed towards the sky as he made his way to the huddle. It was something he always did when they were in a close game.

Ryan was able to complete a few passes to his rookie tight end, Mason, but stalled at the twenty-two yard line. They kicked another field goal increasing their lead 13-6.

Before Ellen knew it there were only two minutes left in the fourth quarter and it was all coming down to this final drive. If San Diego wanted to be crowned world champions, they needed to score a touchdown. Green Bay was up 26-20 after San Diego's defense had shown its exhaustion.

Ryan ran out onto the field, pointing towards the sky again and Ellen almost caught herself whispering a prayer for a score to win the game. She stopped herself, remembering that God didn't listen to her anyway and would probably cause them to lose just to spite her. She folded her hands in her lap, leaning forward in her chair, trying to will all she had into Ryan's game.

Time seemed to tick by too quickly and San Diego only had one time-out remaining. Ryan did his best to manage the clock, but after his tight end, Mason, was tackled in bounds, they had to line up and quickly spike the ball.

Now there were only six seconds left. That left them with time for only one more play and they needed a touchdown. They were on Green Bay's sixteen-yard line, but for Ellen it was more like sixteen miles. She could barely keep her eyes open when the ball was snapped back to Ryan.

He looked left and motioned with his free hand, the rush was coming towards him and Ellen let out a panicked squeal. "Ryan, throw it!" she yelled.

Ryan sidestepped out of tackle and threw the ball towards the end zone. TOUCHDOWN! His wide receiver, Antwon, was there with the clutch catch.

Ellen leaped from her chair, screaming in excitement. The whole team ran onto the field, embracing Antwon and Ryan. The referees were blowing their whistles, signaling everyone to get back on the sideline, so the extra kick could be completed. The score was tied now, so the win was not theirs yet.

San Diego lined up for the extra point and the stadium was blanketed in an eerie silence. Everyone held their breath as the ball traveled through the air and passed through the uprights. The kick was good! San Diego was the Super Bowl champion! Ryan was a Super Bowl champion!

Ellen had tears flowing freely down her cheeks and she didn't care. Ryan did it; Ryan had won the Super Bowl. Ellen watched as confetti fell from the sky covering the team, celebrating in the middle of the field. The media was trying to break in to get interviews, but the inseparable bond the team had formed there in the center of the field impeded their chances.

Ellen stayed there in the press box and watched as the Lombardi trophy was presented to the team. The NFL commissioner stepped onto the podium and talked about the Super Bowl MVP award. "I'm proud to announce that this year's honor goes to quarterback, Ryan Salas!"

Ellen stood and cheered as she watched Ryan accept his award. Her cheeks hurt from all the smiling she was doing, but she couldn't help it. She would never forget this moment. She stayed and listened to his speech before heading back to her hotel. She had an early flight in the morning.

"I want to thank my Savior, first and foremost. He gifted me with these abilities and I am honored to spend each day sharing His glory doing something I love. Secondly, I want to thank my parents for their unending support and encouragement, pushing me to where I am today. Thirdly, I want to thank the San Diego fans, because without you guys we wouldn't be able to do what we do." The stadium erupted in thunderous applause as Ryan stepped from the podium.

Ellen stayed a few minutes longer, soaking up as much of this experience as she could. Her heart was full with all the excitement going on and she didn't want it to end. She gathered up her stuff and made her way out of the stadium and back to her hotel. This was going to be the best article she had ever written in her career.

CHAPTER THIRTY

Ellen squeezed her tea bag, extracting the water into her mug. She took in a deep breath of the calming, blueberry aroma. She tossed the used tea bag into the trashcan and ambled over to her couch. She sat down and curled her legs underneath her, taking a sip of her tea. The warmth coated the back of her throat, soothing the dryness that had been bugging her all day.

She set the mug on her coffee table and reached for her laptop that was sitting on the floor charging. Many things had happened in Ellen's life since her Super Bowl article was published over two years ago. Her boss had deemed it "her best piece ever," and from there he moved Ellen up within the magazine company. She was twenty-six now and had accomplished so much at a young age.

The article had been out of her usual muse, going the route of Ryan's faith and how it had helped the team win the most important game of their lives. Her boss had been leery at first with her trying this approach. "The magazine's reputation is on the line here," he had repeated numerous times. But something had pushed Ellen to take that particular angle and it had paid off.

Ellen logged on to her personal website and spent the next hour reading the comments from people all over the world on her latest articles. Yes, there were some negative and downright rude people out there, but they were overshadowed by all the positive comments that people graciously sent Ellen's way.

She shut her laptop and reached for her mug, curling up into the corner of the couch. She took a few more sips of her blueberry delight tea that had now grown cold. She let her mind wonder, contemplating all that had gone on over the last few years of her life. Her career-launching article had stirred her in a deep way, but the doubts constantly crept into her heart and soul about all that had gone wrong in her earlier years of life. The question of how a so-called, loving God had allowed those things to happen would always plague her. There were days when Eric's accident came flashing back so vividly she wasn't sure she could breathe. Whenever that happened she stood firm in her belief that the faith she once had was all wrong.

Ellen gazed out the large bay window in her apartment's living room, overlooking New York City. A gentle snow fell outside, one last blast from winter before spring came around the corner. She missed the warmth of her hometown. She went and visited her parents as often as she could. She had even tried to convince them to come and live with her here in New York, but they were content to remain in their little beachside cottage. Ellen didn't blame them. The slow-paced, beach life was wonderful and there were days when the craziness of New York would get to Ellen. She still loved New York though. There was no other place that held this kind of vibrancy. Ellen glanced out the window again, admiring the white flakes. Snow had been a foreign object to her, having grown up in the south all of her life, but she had grown accustomed to the cold and enjoyed the still silence a peaceful snowfall gave to the city. This storm wasn't supposed to amount to much, but Ellen enjoyed watching the snowflakes meander down from their home in the sky to the sidewalks and streets below.

A soft knock sounded at her door and Ellen pulled herself from her comfortable seat to go see who it was. She tightened her ponytail and straightened her t-shirt as she walked towards the door, trying to make her appearance somewhat presentable for whoever it was that was there. She had been seeing a guy named Brent lately, but things hadn't been going well with him, so Ellen was pretty sure it wasn't Brent at the door. There wasn't anything wrong with Brent, he was a very sweet guy, but Ellen didn't feel any romantic connection. She knew she needed to break things off with him, but she enjoyed his company and was reluctant to let him go, for that reason. Hopefully, he would be open to the idea of just maintaining a close friendship between them and the awkwardness of romantic advancement would dwindle.

The door creaked slightly as she pulled it open to reveal her surprise visitor. "Katie! It's so good to see you! I didn't know you were coming for a visit." Ellen hugged her friend, thankful to see her.

Ellen let go and motioned for her friend to walk inside. Katie had only been up to visit her twice before while Ellen had been in New York. Sadly, their chaotic lives had made it difficult to maintain frequent visits with each other.

"I wanted to surprise you." Katie's face was beaming as she hugged Ellen again. "It's been too long and I couldn't go on living another day without seeing your face."

Ellen laughed at her friend's dramatic words, even

though Ellen felt exactly the same way.

Katie plopped down on Ellen's couch. "So, tell me about your exciting, famous life. Still as grand as ever?" Katie slid her shoes off and pulled her feet underneath her. Her blond hair was cut shorter than the last time Ellen had seen her and it framed her face, accentuating its shape beautifully.

Ellen sat down next to her friend. "Yes, it's still as grand as ever. Have you been keeping up with my latest work?"

"Girl, you know I read everything you write. With everything I have going on in life how would I keep up with the sports' world if it wasn't for you?"

"As always, I'm glad I can keep you in the loop." Both girls laughed.

"You should be proud. You have a God-given talent that should not be wasted. You show that talent to the world my friend!" Katie exclaimed.

Ellen smiled at her friend's exuberance. She kept Ellen going on a daily basis with her encouraging texts and phone calls and even though they didn't see each other face to face very often, she felt Katie's presence every day.

"So, I have some news to add to my list of life adventures." Katie had done a lot of traveling over the last couple of years and Ellen assumed she was going on another journey.

"Where to this time, my friend?" Ellen asked.

"It's not 'where', it's 'who'," Katie said coyly.

"Who?" Ellen was confused. She stared at her friend blankly, waiting for her to explain.

Katie moved her left hand from her lap and lifted it so Ellen could see it. "Adam and I are getting married!"

Ellen reached for Katie's hand and jumped off the couch. They both began squealing in joy. "Oh my gosh, I'm so happy for you Katie!" Ellen stopped jumping and hugged her friend. She let go and reached for Katie's hand again, admiring the stunning ring. "It's beautiful. He did a wonderful job picking it out."

"Well, actually, I told him what to get, but at least he didn't forget what I told him." Katie was beaming from ear to ear.

They chatted about the proposal and Ellen's eyes watered as she heard the story. It was so romantic. Straight from a movie screen. A tinge of jealousy hit Ellen as she thought back on the day of her own proposal. Sadly, it didn't end like Katie's had. She quickly wiped that memory from her thoughts and focused on celebrating with her friend.

"Let's go down to Letuca's for some food and drinks and celebrate this occasion!"

"That sounds wonderful. I loved their food the last time I was here." Katie clapped her hands together, sheer joy pouring from her.

"Let me change into more appropriate attire and then we'll head out." Ellen made her way back to her bedroom to find a new outfit to wear.

A few minutes later, the girls made their way outside and walked the few blocks to Letuca's. It was a sports bar that Ellen always enjoyed going to. Pete, the restaurant's owner, was a fan of hers. Luckily, it wasn't too cold and the snow had stopped falling for the time being, as they made their way there.

The girls found a table towards the back, quiet enough for them to continue talking without shouting at each other. They each ordered a strawberry margarita and a "Letuca's special" burger. Pete said, "The 'special' was in the sauce." Whatever it was, Ellen loved it.

"The main reason I came here in person to tell you about the engagement is because I had a special question to ask you."

Ellen swallowed her bite of burger, "What is it?"

Katie reached across the table and took Ellen's hand, "Ellie, will you be my maid of honor? I can't think of anyone else I would want to be standing next to me on my special day."

"Of course! I wouldn't miss it for the world. You're my best friend and I couldn't imagine anything better." Ellen squeezed Katie's hand and they both continued to talk about the wedding and everything else going on in each other's lives. Ellen's heart was glad, and along with her full stomach, she was feeling thankful that her best friend had stopped by for this unexpected visit.

Just as the girls were getting ready to leave and head back to Ellen's apartment Katie pointed to a television located behind Ellen. "Ellie, turn around!" Her voice was panicky.

Ellen wheeled around quickly and focused on the screen. A picture of Ryan was in the top left corner and the main screen had a reporter speaking, red and blue lights were flashing in the background. The headline read NFL STAR, RYAN SALAS, INVOLVED IN DEVASTATING CRASH. Ellen froze; the whole restaurant went silent as everyone focused their attention on the screen. *No, this could not be happening again.*

"Ellie, you need to go to him. Right now." Katie whispered.

CHAPTER THIRTY-ONE

After they had sprinted the few blocks back to Ellen's apartment, Katie tried her best to keep Ellen calm and thinking clearly.

"You're going to need summer clothes in California. Make sure you pack shorts." Katie gave Ellen instructions, trying to keep her focused.

Ellen couldn't focus though. Everything in her was screaming in fear. Why was this happening to her again?

She went through a series of motions, packing her suitcase and gathering what she needed. She traveled around the country often with her job, interviewing players and gathering information that she needed for her writing assignments, so everything she needed was already organized.

Katie hugged her as they parted ways, letting her know that she was praying for her and wanted updates as soon as Ellen had them.

Ellen turned and got in the cab, heading to the airport. She had booked the earliest flight to San Diego that she could find online and had about an hour to spare. She told the taxi driver to go as fast as he could.

Ellen kept checking her phone, trying to see if there were any updates on Ryan's condition. She also wanted to know what had caused the accident and frequently looked for updates on that as well. Ellen had covered a story like this about a year and a half ago, and she knew how intense the situation would be. Luckily, the New York player that had been in the accident had pulled through and was still playing in the NFL today. However, this was Ryan, her Ryan, and as hard as it was to admit, she still loved him. She had never stopped loving him. Every fiber in her body ached for a second chance. A part of her almost whispered a prayer, but she stopped herself, knowing that it would only be ignored.

The drive to the airport went quickly, which Ellen was grateful for, because she did not have a lot of time to catch her plane. She checked her one bag and raced to security, willing the line to move faster. She was constantly checking her phone, but still no word. She had even texted a few contacts of hers in San Diego, hoping they would be able to feed her the inside scoop until she got there. None of them had any news for her, but they all said they would let her know about anything they heard as soon as they could.

Ellen made it through security and sat down in a seat at her gate. The plane wasn't boarding yet, but she had secured a first class seat with her writing clearances, so she would be boarding any minute now.

The flight seemed like it was taking an eternity. Ellen wanted the plane to fly faster, but it felt like it was crawling at a snail's pace. Didn't these people understand the emergent situation she was in?

A few people came up to her and asked for her autograph, telling her how much they enjoyed her work. She happily obliged them, but her insides were shredded into pieces and she wasn't really in a mood to talk to anyone.

The plane finally landed in San Diego and Ellen rushed through that airport as well. She felt like she could not get to Ryan fast enough. She had checked her phone after the plane landed and saw that the only update was that Ryan was in critical condition. She was just thankful he was alive at this point. She pushed her way past people, not caring how rude she was being. She had somewhere to be and these people were hindering her progress in getting there.

She called for a taxi when she finally got outside the airport. She directed him to the hospital where her one contact had told her Ryan was located. She slipped off her sweatshirt and shoved it into her oversized purse. It was humid in San Diego even though it was very early in the morning. She gazed up at the stars as the taxi driver made his way to the hospital, the sun still waiting to make its appearance for the day.

As she watched the blackness slowly dissipate, it took her back to the many times her and Ryan had sat on their field and watched the stars together. If she had the ability to rewind time she would go back to one of those moments and savor it just a little more. She would take in the details of his face, melt into his kiss a little longer and be thankful for the man she had in her life. That was all gone now, because of her, and she regretted it every day of her life. Sure, she had dated some guys over the years, but none of them had worked out. She found herself comparing all of them to Ryan, even though she tried not to, but every single one of them fell short of her expectations.

She sighed as she leaned her head against the window, if only she could turn back time and undo what she had done.

The hospital came into view and she grabbed her suitcase from the taxi's trunk when the driver pulled up to the curb. She paid and thanked the man and ran towards the glass doors. She really wished she had stopped at a hotel first to drop off her suitcase, but she obviously wasn't thinking clearly. She'd just have to lug it around for now. She jogged up to the receptionist desk, her suitcase in tow and stated her reason for being there. "I'm here to see Ryan Salas. My name is Ellen Kane. I'm a very close friend of his."

The receptionist smiled and her dark blue eyes even sparkled, which Ellen didn't understand. This was not a situation to be smiling about.

"I thought I recognized you. I enjoy reading your articles. I've never been a big football fan, but after reading your work I've come to enjoy it." She was typing slowly on her keyboard. Ellen wanted to shout at her to hurry up and stop talking, but she knew that was not going to help the situation.

"He's in the emergency wing, but he is not allowed any visitors at this time. You are welcome to sit in the waiting room until something changes."

Ellen thanked the blonde haired woman and headed down the hallway until she found the emergency section of the hospital. It was a longer walk than she had anticipated and her suitcase was really becoming quite a burden. She wasn't stopping now; she was so close to him. She would just sit and wait until she heard anything new.

She rounded another corner and with each step, her anxiety grew. *What if he didn't live through this?* She chided herself; she couldn't start thinking that way. *Positive. Stay positive,* she whispered to herself with each step she took.

The waiting room for the emergency wing finally came

into view. Ellen felt like she had reached the final stretch of a very long race; the outcome wasn't a medal though.

A couple stood up as she came closer and they started walking towards her. *Oh great, more fans.* Ellen was not in the mood for this right now. As the couple made their way closer to Ellen, a familiarity washed over her. It was Ryan's parents.

No one said a word; all Ellen could do was run the final few feet towards them and hug them. All the tears she had been holding back since she heard the news started flowing now. Ellen didn't care. They stood there as a group for a long time, trying to draw strength from each other just to get through this.

Rick and June shared what they knew with Ellen, most of it being information Ellen had already heard from her contacts. Ryan had been on his way to a party at Antwon's, his wide receiver's house. A driver had blown through a red light, hitting Ryan's driver side door and all but crushing Ryan. As the receptionist had said, his parents informed Ellen of his critical condition. "The doctor is very optimistic; especially because it's a miracle he even survived the accident." More tears surfaced and fell down June's face. "I'm just praying my baby will pull through this."

Ellen pulled her in for another hug. They all returned to the waiting area and sat down in some chairs that were away from the other people. Silence followed as they patiently waited to hear updates from the doctor. Ellen was surprised the media wasn't swarming the place, especially with such a high profile player like Ryan involved. Ellen just figured the hospital was directing them away for now.

A few hours passed and still no word from the doctor. Ellen could barely keep her eyes open at this point, even though the sun was streaming through the windows, brightening the entire waiting room. It did little to brighten Ellen's mood though. With each hour that passed, Ellen felt Ryan was slipping further and further away.

Ryan's doctor finally rounded the corner, "He seems to be making some improvements, albeit very small improvements, but he's in a room now that you can go and see him. He is still unconscious, but we need him to be, for now, until the swelling of his brain begins to decrease."

Ellen didn't understand that, but she wasn't in the medical profession, so who was she to question what the doctor was doing or saying. Still dragging her suitcase along with her, she followed the doctor and Ryan's parents back to the private room where he was located.

Ellen's hand flew to her mouth when she saw him. He was bandaged practically from head to toe; his left leg was elevated and in a cast. What little you could see of his face was cut up and swollen. Tears started falling rapidly as she took in Ryan's condition. The doctor was explaining things to Ryan's parents, but Ellen didn't hear a word of it. All she could do was stare at Ryan. Flashbacks of Eric lying in a hospital bed came screaming back at her. It was as if she were reliving that nightmare all over again.

~*~

One Month Later...

Still no change... Ellen was falling deeper into a pit of despair with each passing day. The doctor came in and said the same thing every day and Ellen was sick of it. Wasn't there anything they could do to help him, to bring Ryan back? He needed to wake up.

Every day Ellen sat by his bedside for as long as she was allowed to. Then she would spend time with her parents and Ryan's parents for the remainder of each day. She tried to focus on work, but it was difficult with everything going on. Her boss understood and was giving her a ton of leniency, but he still expected her to submit articles when she could. So far, she had managed to squeak out one piece and Jim had liked it, so thankfully it appeased him for the time being, before she had to start focusing on another one.

Ellen turned to Ryan and stroked his arm. She talked to him all the time, hoping he'd hear her, but there was still no response. She'd probably apologized about a thousand times at this point, but it didn't matter. It would only matter if he woke up and actually heard her, responded to her in person, fully conscious.

CHAPTER THIRTY-TWO

The rain came down in torrents outside, dampening Ellen's mood with each passing hour. The doctor had come in a little while ago, saying the same thing, as usual. Ellen leaned forward in her chair; her paper cup full of coffee warmed her hands. The coffee did little to keep her awake, but it was something. Ryan's parents had stopped by earlier in the morning and just like Ellen, they were growing weary of the doctor repeating the same thing day after day.

Ellen got up from her chair and walked over to the lone window in Ryan's room. The raindrops trailed one after the other in a race to the bottom of the glass. Ellen took her finger and mindlessly traced one of the trails, wishing for a change in Ryan. Each day was becoming a mindless blur. The longer Ryan went being unconscious, the more worried Ellen and everyone else became.

Ellen walked back over to her chair and tossed her empty coffee cup in the trashcan. She was going to have to make her way back downstairs for another cup. One had not been enough for her today. She had never been a big coffee drinker before, but with everything going on lately, it became a routine.

Ryan's parents had brought Ryan's bible in earlier that morning. It was on the small table next to Ryan's bed. Ellen's eyes focused on it. She didn't have anything else to do so she picked it up. It felt strange in her hands, but familiar all at the same time. The pages shimmered in what little light was in the room. Ellen flipped open to the first page, which had Ryan's name inscribed on it and the date he had received it. Ellen looked through the table of contents, recognizing many of the books from when she was a child: Genesis, Psalms and Proverbs. The Gospels as well. It all came rushing back to her. The Sunday school days and church picnics. She missed those days, but after everything that had happened to her, she just couldn't get past the hurt and the doubts. She wanted to close the Bible and put it back on the table, but something kept her from doing that. It was like an invisible hand pushing her forward, nudging her in the shoulder to read on.

She skimmed through some pages, unsure of where or what to focus on. She stopped in the book of Job. She vaguely remembered the story from childhood, but she decided to read it again. She had nothing else planned for the day, so some reading seemed like a productive activity.

She curled her feet underneath her and tried to get as comfortable as she could in the stiff hospital chair. She started from the beginning in the story of Job and really got into it the more she read. Job had lost everything, but remained grounded in his faith, giving praise to God through it all. Ellen felt a sense of disbelief trying to figure out how someone who had lost everything, literally everything in his life, could still maintain an unwavering faith. In the end, God blessed him with even more than Job had before. Ellen closed the Bible and glanced up at the clock. She was shocked to see a little over two hours had passed. She had been so focused on reading she didn't bother to ever check on the time. Her stomach grumbled and she decided to head down to the cafeteria for something to eat.

Ryan's parents stopped by and joined her at the table she was eating at. Ellen shared with them what she had read in Ryan's bible and how it had made her start thinking about some things. June smiled and hugged Ellen tight, "I'm so glad to hear this sweetie." June started going on and on about faith, God, and life. Ellen didn't have the heart to tell her that her feelings hadn't changed towards God, but she also wasn't opposed to anything. She still had a long way to go, but for Ryan's sake, she thought she would give it a try.

She ate the rest of her lunch while Rick and June went up to visit with their son for a little bit. Ellen wanted them to have their time alone with him so she decided to get some errands done and then visit with Ryan later that evening before visiting hours were over.

Ellen returned later that night, found her spot in the chair again and reached for Ryan's bible. Something was pulling at her heart and she wanted to continue reading. She flipped to the back of the book and looked through the section about peace, something she had been without for the past month. A list of verses appeared underneath the word and Ellen jotted them down in the notebook on her phone. She started with the first one listed, Psalm 10:17. It took a little while to locate, but she was slowly getting the hang of it.

Ellen scrolled down the page and located the verse, *"You, Lord, hear the desire of the afflicted; You encourage them and You listen to their cry."* Ellen read that verse again. A small spark resonated in her and she tried to focus on the words. She had refused to pray ever since Eric died, thinking God wouldn't listen to her, but here in this verse it said He listened to her cry and encouraged her.

Ellen kept moving through the list, locating the next verse, Isaiah 41:10. *"So, do not fear for I am with you; do not be dismayed for I am your God. I will strengthen you and help you. I will uphold you in my righteous right hand."*

Ellen felt a lump growing in her throat. It was as if God himself were standing right here in front of her, talking directly to her about the situation she was in right now.

Ellen kept going through the list reading each verse. Peace was wrapping itself around her heart and soul and she felt as if she were coming home after a long journey through a lonely desert. John 16:33 was next on her list, *"I have told you these things, so that in Me you may have peace. In this world, you will have trouble, but take heart! I have overcome the world."* The lump was growing larger with each verse she read. She was trying to hold it back, but something powerful was happening and she couldn't stop it.

She was down to the last one on her list and tears had already started falling, leaving marks on the pages. This book was a part of Ryan and with each verse she read, she felt like she was reading about who he was. God had been the sole focus of Ryan's life and in his career; Ellen was now beginning to understand. She wasn't perfect, no one was, but what she was getting out of this little revival session of hers was a type of peace that she had never experienced before. A deep cleansing of her soul that she had needed since the day she had lost hope and suppressed her faith. Before she read the last verse, she closed her eyes and thought back to the day she stood by Eric's casket. She had been so angry with God that day. He had taken her best friend away from her. No, she would never understand why, but as it said in John, this world was not perfect and there would be trials and heartbreak that everyone would go through. God is the strength we are supposed to pull from in those times. She pictured Eric's grandma that day and what she had said to Ellen before she left. It made sense now.

She glanced down at Matthew 11:28, "*Come to me all you who are weary and heavily burdened and I will give you rest.*" That's when the dam broke and the sobs came. Everything Ellen had been holding back had burst and she wasn't ashamed. God had never left her all this time; she had left Him. Here He was offering her rest through everything she had been through. He was holding out His hand telling her to take it and He would lead her through the darkness. But she had refused; she had slapped His hand away and rejected Him. Just a few verses had broken down the walls built around her heart. She was breaking, but she was breaking in a good way. Her selfishness was crumbling and God's peace was filling her completely. She reached for the tissues on the table by Ryan's bed and dabbed at her eyes. The tears continued to come, but it felt good. God was cleansing her soul.

She leaned back in the chair, the bible still open in her lap. *God, I know it's been too long and I'm sorry. I'm sorry for rejecting you, for trying to do things on my own strength. I'm sorry for blaming you. I know this may seem like a long shot, but I know you're at least listening. Please, please heal Ryan. I can't bear to lose him. He has so much life ahead of him yet to live. I need him back God and I know you know that. I finally realize the importance of his faith now that I share it with him and I want more than anything for him to know that. I want him to know God. Please grant me the opportunity to tell him.* She wasn't sure how to end the prayer so she just stopped talking. A huge weight had been lifted from her and she felt calm, more so than she had felt in a very long time.

~*~

Her hair was darker than the last time he had seen her and he liked it. She was so beautiful. Time had blessed her. He wasn't sure why she was crying, maybe because of him. He wasn't sure. He watched as she dabbed her eyes with the tissue. She flipped a page in the book that was on her lap and he blinked to adjust his eyes. It was his bible. Ellen was reading his bible? His heart started to race. He had been praying for this moment for years. Has it finally been answered? Was Ellen rediscovering her faith? He smiled as he watched her, overjoyed and flooded with love for her.

A few seconds later, she turned towards him and her eyes grew large. Her hand flew to her mouth in shock as she said his name, "Ryan!"

CHAPTER THIRTY-THREE

Ellen wiped the final tear from her face and turned to glance at Ryan one last time, before she had to leave for the night. When she looked over his eyes were open and he was watching her. Her hand flew to her mouth in shock as she exclaimed, "Ryan!"

She jumped from her chair and fell onto her knees next to his bed so that she was eye level with him. She took in the sight of him as she held onto his hand. The cuts on his face were healing and the swelling had gone way down. Their eyes locked, but no words were needed. In that moment, Ellen felt like her whole world had finally come together. Ryan was living and breathing and she was right there with him, living and breathing in a whole new way.

He tried to speak, but his voice was severely hoarse. Ellen put her finger to his lips, "Save your voice."

Ellen pressed the nurse call button and a plump, blonde-haired woman entered a few seconds later. "Well, it looks like someone is finally awake. I'll call the doctor so he can come examine you." She jotted some things down on her clipboard and scurried out of the room to get the doctor.

Dr. Brennan came in a few minutes later and checked a

bunch of different things. Ellen sat nervously in her chair, waiting to hear what he had to say. Yes, Ryan was awake, but Dr. Brennan had said, before he started the exam, that it didn't mean he was out of the woods quite yet.

He asked Ryan a series of questions about the accident and events from the past. Ellen assumed it was to test his memory retention and so far, he had answered everything correctly. His voice was extremely raspy, but Ellen was just thankful he was talking. The doctor checked Ryan's reflexes and did a lot of head nodding. Ellen wished he would explain what he was doing instead of being so silent, but she let him do his job. She had called both her parents and Ryan's parents to let them know the great news. They should be arriving any minute now. Hopefully, Dr. Brennan would be finished by then and be able to share his prognosis with all of them.

Rick and June showed up first, tears filling both of their eyes. Their son was awake after a long, stressful month of worry and prayer. Colt and Meredith showed up shortly thereafter and hugs were exchanged between the group. All of them were experiencing an overwhelming joy.

The doctor stepped out of the room for a second to discuss something with the blonde-haired nurse. She smiled, nodded and walked down the hallway and Ellen took that as a sign of very good news to come.

Ellen, her parents, and Ryan's parents all gathered in a small circle in the hallway, anxiously waiting for the doctor's news.

Dr. Brennan coughed to clear his throat and smiled at them, "Well, I'm happy to say, it looks like Ryan will be making a full recovery. His memory seems to be perfectly fine and nothing has been neurologically affected by the accident. We will be moving him downstairs shortly into a general room and then we will be keeping him the rest of the week to monitor him.

They all grasped each other in a big hug, thankful that Ryan was going to be okay. Rick sent up a quick prayer of thanks and Ellen gladly joined in. She had never felt this much joy in her life. After all these years of harboring anger towards God, He had answered her prayer to bring Ryan back. She was beyond grateful. She voiced her own silent prayer of thanks after Rick finished his.

"Before you all go I wanted to let you know one final thing. I'll be telling Ryan later, after he gets some rest, but I wanted to give you a heads up beforehand. Due to the severity of the accident and the toll it has taken on Ryan's neck and back; he will no longer be able to play football." Dr. Brennan turned and headed down the hallway, as if his last little bit of news was perfectly normal. Ellen stood there in shock, as did everyone else. How was Ryan going to take that? Football was his passion.

The five of them stood in the hallway, silence taking over. No one was sure how to take the news and all of them knew how devastating the blow would be to Ryan.

The news spread quickly through the media that Ryan was alive and well. Paparazzi was flooding the hospital and Ryan was being bombarded with interviews. Dr. Brennan limited the number of people during the day, stating Ryan needed his rest to recover fully. Nothing was said to the media about his football career being over, but Ryan was having trouble accepting the news. He was frustrated, disappointed and angry. Ellen admired him though, because even though he was devastated, he knew and believed God had an ultimate plan for him.

Ellen and Ryan hadn't had a private moment since Ryan came out of his coma, but this afternoon Ellen was finally going to get her chance.

She opened his door quietly and stepped into the room. He was propped up on some pillows, watching television. "Hey you," she said to him.

"Hey," he reached for the remote to turn the television off and patted a spot on the bed for her to sit next to him. "I've wanted to talk to you."

Ellen smiled as she walked over to him and took the seat he had offered her. "I've wanted to talk to you too."

Ryan pointed to her, "You first."

Ellen inhaled a deep breath and prepared herself. She had been praying for this moment and now that it was here, she was nervous. "Well, for starters, I'm so glad you're okay. When I saw the accident on the news I flew out here as quickly as I could." Ellen swallowed the lump in her throat. She couldn't cry, not yet anyway. She had a lot to say.

She cleared her throat and spoke, "Ryan, I'm sorry. I'm sorry for everything. I haven't been able to forgive myself for what I did to you. I ruined us. I wish I could take it all back, I wish I had the ability to go back in time and undo everything." A tear escaped over her eyelid and ran down her cheek, but she took another deep breath. She had to keep going, get everything out.

"I never stopped loving you. Every interview I watched and every game that I cheered you on, the love was still there. Every. Single. Time. You were the greatest thing that ever happened to me. You inspire me; you pushed me towards my dreams, which I achieved. It's all because of you. I found God again, because of you too. Your faith inspired me, Ryan." A sob escaped her lips and more tears began to fall. "If you can find it in your heart to forgive me, I'd finally be able to move on," she squeaked out. "As I've said before, you deserve so much better than me, but if we could somehow find a way back, even if only to friendship, I would be more than happy."

Ryan leaned forward and wiped the tears from Ellen's cheek. His voice was still a little raspy, but Ellen could hear him as clear as day. "Ellen, I forgave you a long time ago. I forgave you that day. I don't want a friendship with you though." Ryan took her hands in his, "I want a relationship with you Ellen. I want a life together. There wasn't a single day that I stopped praying for this moment. Ellen, I haven't stopped loving you either. Never have and never will. As I told you all those years ago, I plan on loving you forever."

He pulled her close to him then and kissed her. Kissed her with the love that never left either one of them, with a passion that would tie them together for life. Their tears mingled together as they continued that kiss, a kiss that had been a long time coming.

Ellen pulled away for a second and looked into his vibrant, green eyes that she had missed dearly. "You have no idea how much those words mean to me. I love you Ryan and I plan on it being forever too." She leaned in and kissed him again, thanking God that this wonderful man was back in her life.

~*~

Ryan prepared himself for the inevitable, his retirement press conference. He had been preparing his speech for the last couple of weeks and the day was finally here. He would never be ready; he was walking away from his passion. Football had been his whole life. There would be other opportunities, but it would never amount to the excitement of actually playing the sport. His agent, Michael, stepped into the room. "You're on in ten."

"Thanks. Can I talk to you for a second?"

"Sure," Michael took a seat in the chair across from Ryan.

"I just wanted to tell you thanks for everything you have done for me over the years. I wouldn't have had the success I did if it weren't for you." Ryan reached for Michael's hand, but Michael pushed it away and gave Ryan a hug instead.

"It's been an honor being your agent during your career. You've taught me a lot and I'm thankful for it all. Let's go out there and knock this speech out of the park." Ryan patted Michael on the back and the two of them headed out to where the podium was set for Ryan.

The NFL commissioner was finishing his speech as Ryan watched from the background. His heart was racing and he prayed that God would give him the strength to make it through this.

His name was called and he stepped up to the podium, glancing down to see Ellen smiling at him from the front row. Each day that passed with her back in his life was a miracle. She looked so beautiful in her teal dress. She had her notebook in her lap along with her voice recorder, as she prepared to work on her final piece for Magnitude magazine. She was moving back to South Carolina with her parents until they figured out what they were doing next in life. Ryan had a few coaching offers on the table from a few teams, but they both wanted to take a break from their careers and spend time together catching up and planning for the future.

Ryan cleared his throat and began his speech. Everyone sat silently as he reflected on the highs and lows of his career, his favorite moments and his regrets. He acknowledged his teammates and how much they meant to him, not only as teammates, but also as good friends. He thanked his coaches and San Diego's owner for their belief in him and the opportunity they provided him to play in San Diego. He answered a few questions from the media and concluded his speech with his favorite verse, 1 Timothy 4:7, *"I have fought the good fight. I have finished the race. I have kept the faith."*

Applauding and cheers ensued as Ryan stepped from the podium. Flashes from the cameras lit the room as Ryan held up his San Diego jersey. He smiled proudly, even though inside he was breaking. He was going to miss this place.

CHAPTER THIRTY-FOUR

The warm, salty breeze blew through her bedroom window as she finished her hair and makeup. Ellen smiled at herself in the mirror, satisfied with the result. Katie was getting married today and she was excited for her dear friend. The ceremony would be at dusk in a local garden that went well with Katie's elegant theme. The flowers would bring a fairytale-like beauty to the sacred moment. The ceremony would not be a large one, just close family and friends and Ellen was honored to be standing beside Katie on her special day.

Ryan would be picking her up soon and taking her to the gardens. There was a little guesthouse on the property where the girls would be getting ready. Ellen gathered up her hair and makeup supplies and put them in her bag. She was the designated hair and makeup artist for the day. Katie did not want to spend money on a professional when she felt Ellen's abilities were just as good. She'd rather save that money for some fun excursions on her and Adam's Bahama honeymoon.

Ellen glanced around her room to make sure she had

everything and walked into her parents' living room to wait for Ryan. Her dad was sitting on the couch reading the local paper. "You look stunning my dear," he said as he put the paper down on the coffee table, and patted the spot next to him on the couch. "Is Katie ready for her big day?"

Ellen took the seat next to her dad, "She's more than ready. She's been waiting for this day for a very long time."

Colt smiled at his daughter, "I believe you'll be next."

Ellen chuckled. She'd been dreaming of her own wedding day since she was a little girl and she and Ryan had been discussing their future plans together. Because of the lengthy time apart from each other, they had been taking their time rekindling their relationship. It had only been six months since he had come out of his coma and Ellen was content with where they were in life. Yes, she wanted to marry Ryan, wanted him to be her husband, but after what happened during his last proposal, she understood the reluctance to take that step forward.

She saw his Jeep pull into the driveway and got up from her spot next to her dad. "I'll see you and mom at the wedding in a few hours." Her dad nodded and went back to his newspaper.

Ryan's Jeep was a newer model of the one he had back in the day. This one was navy blue. Ellen threw her bag into the back of the Jeep and hopped into the passenger seat.

"You look gorgeous babe." Ryan leaned over and kissed her softly on the cheek, knowing she wouldn't want her makeup smeared.

"Thank you." Ellen looked Ryan up and down, taking in his appearance. He wore khaki slacks with a light grey, button-down shirt. His sleeves were rolled mid-way up his forearms. His hair was freshly cut and his blue eyes sparkled in the sunlight. He was so handsome. Ellen was thankful for the blessing of having Ryan back in her life. It was a dream come true for her.

They made their way to the gardens where Adam and Katie's wedding was going to take place, singing along to songs on the radio and laughing. Ellen felt so carefree in this moment. She wouldn't trade this time in her life for anything.

They arrived half an hour later and Ellen walked across the grounds to the guesthouse. Katie sat perched on a chair, chatting away about every little wedding detail. When Ellen walked in the door, Katie jumped up and squealed. "Ellie! Can you believe it? My day is finally here!"

Ellen embraced her friend and joined in on the squeals of excitement. Katie's soon-to-be sister-in-law, Amber, was the only other girl in the wedding party. Ellen had met her once before. She was a quiet, reserved person, but today she was just as joyful and talkative as Katie was. Katie's mom and soon-to-be mother-in-law were also in the room.

Ellen got started on Katie's hair, knowing time would pass quickly. She didn't want to be rushed, so she wanted to start right away. She curled Katie's shimmery, blond locks and began pinning layers with bobby pins into a sophisticated up do. The final bobby pins had little white flowers attached to the ends, which Ellen used to pin up some of the loose strands. She allowed some curls to hang down, shaping Katie's face. She got started on Katie's makeup next, keeping everything neutral and earthy looking. She added a pop of lavender in Katie's eye shadow to make her eyes stand out.

"Adam is going to faint when he sees you. You look absolutely gorgeous, my friend." Ellen stepped back and allowed Katie to admire herself in the mirror.

"Ellen, everything looks so pretty! I love it! My hair, makeup, everything!" Katie was beaming from ear to ear, touching her hair gently and moving closer to the mirror to take in the details. "Thank you so much." She stood and hugged her friend. "Thank you for being here today. It means the world to me."

"Don't go making us both cry." Ellen protested. "I don't have time to fix our makeup!" Both girls laughed and hugged again.

"Seriously though, I'm honored to be part of your special day." Ellen said as she pulled away from the hug.

Katie smiled and turned to go grab their dresses.

Ellen's dress was a lavender shade that matched Katie's eye shadow and Amber's was a darker purple. Katie's dress was a simple gown, but the intricate lace details made it stunning.

Ellen slipped into her dress and then helped Katie slide into hers and zipped up the back. Ellen put her hand to her mouth as her friend turned around. "Katie, you look like you stepped straight out of a magazine." The other women nodded in agreement.

"I do look pretty fantastic, if I do say so myself." Katie winked and did a little curtsy.

The women chuckled and gathered together for a moment of prayer before Katie made her way down the aisle to her future husband.

Katie had found a deep faith after she met Adam and Ellen was thankful that the two of them could share that faith. It was another bond between them that made their friendship unbreakable.

After a quick prayer, Katie grabbed her bouquet of peach colored roses and took a deep breath. "Here goes nothing." She stepped out and met her dad on the lawn. He took her arm and dabbed at a few tears with his handkerchief. Ellen held back her own tears, trying to keep some composure, but everything about this moment was precious. She found herself picturing her and her dad in this moment together. It would be cherished forever.

The violin music began to play and Amber made her way down the cobblestone aisle towards her brother. Ellen was next and began walking forward, the intensity of the moment causing her heart to race. Her best friend was getting married. She made it to the front and smiled at Adam, who was grinning. The love he had for Katie was genuine; Ellen could see it in his eyes.

As the music changed and Katie rounded the corner, Adam's eyes lit up. The groom's reaction was always a sight to see and Ellen was glad she had noticed it. He swiped at a single tear that escaped down his cheek as he watched his bride walk to him in all her fairytale-like radiance.

Katie's dad kissed her cheek and he placed her hand in Adam's. The pastor began his message and Ellen soaked up every moment. The mixing of the sand, the vows, the 'I do's' and of course the first kiss. Applause and cheers erupted as Adam and Katie walked back down the aisle as husband and wife. The setting sun cast a romantic glow on their exit and Ellen carefully wiped a few tears from her face.

The rest of the evening flew by in a flash. The dancing, the cake cutting and the sparkler send-off for the happy couple. It was a day Ellen would never forget.

After the festivities were over Ellen walked back to the guesthouse to change back into her normal clothing and carefully put her dress back into its bag. She gathered up her hair and makeup supplies and walked back outside.

The evening was warm and Ellen slowed her pace to enjoy it. New York had been wonderful, but there was something about this place, the slow pace of living, that spoke to her heart every time.

Ellen found Ryan in the parking lot standing next to his Jeep. "You know what I'm happy about?"

"What's that?" Ellen asked, as she tossed her stuff in the back.

He eyed her up and down, "I'm dating the hottest maid of honor I've ever seen." He swept her off her feet and spun her around, kissing her softly on the lips. He placed her back on the ground and wrapped his arms around her waist, pulling her close to him. "And now that you don't have to worry about your makeup getting smeared I can kiss you like I've wanted to kiss you all day." He put his hands on the back of her head and pulled her close, kissing her with a passion that made Ellen's knees weak. She felt herself melting into the kiss. He pulled away slowly and whispered, "I thank God for you every day Ellie, and someday soon I'll be able to show you how much I love you." He kissed her again and then helped her into the passenger seat of the Jeep.

Ellen's heart was beating fast and she could not stop smiling. When Ryan got into the Jeep and started the engine, she placed her hand on his thigh. "I thank God for you every day too." He took her hand and lifted it to his lips, kissing her fingers. He held on until they reached her parents' house.

"Remember, I'm taking you horseback riding at my Aunt and Uncle's ranch next weekend."

"Yes, I remember. I can't wait." She leaned in and kissed him and then grabbed her stuff from the back. She opened her door and stepped out, walking towards her parents' front porch. She turned and waved at him as he pulled out of the driveway. She felt like that young college girl again, all giddy and in love.

CHAPTER THIRTY-FIVE

The sun was shining bright now, bringing with it the promise of a wonderful day. Ryan and Ellen were on their way to Ryan's Aunt and Uncle's ranch. It was about a three-hour drive from her parents' place, so they got an early start. It allowed them to see the beautiful sunrise, the golden hues turning the dark skies to light. Ellen dozed off for about a half an hour after that, but was now wide-awake and ready to enjoy their day together.

Ellen hadn't been horseback riding since Ryan took her there many years ago, so she was looking forward to the adventure. Plus, with this being family property, there was no need to worry about the paparazzi following them. Ryan had been retired from the NFL for a few months, but he was still a famous icon, even in the state of South Carolina.

Ellen glanced over at him; he was intently focused on the road. His face had some stubble on it, giving him a rugged look. She loved him a lot; there was no denying that. They were infatuated with each other. Even more so than when they were college sweethearts. Ellen felt a stronger, deeper connection this time around. He turned to her then, must have sensed her staring and mouthed the words 'I love you' since the radio was blaring.

A song they both loved came on next and they joined in, in a not so harmonic rendition, but they didn't care. The song finished and they laughed, enjoying their out of tune version even better than the original song. Ryan reached and turned the radio down so he could speak. The wind was whipping through the open windows of the Jeep, so he still had to talk a little louder than usual. "I'm so excited for today. I feel like we are almost stepping back in time and redoing a date, but this time we'll make it even better." He winked at her.

She wasn't sure what he meant by that, but she was all for making new and exciting memories with him. The rest of their drive was uneventful. A lot of handholding and starry-eyed looks passed between them until they finally pulled up to the gate for the Heart and Soul Ranch.

Ryan parked the Jeep near the barn, which hadn't changed a bit since the last time Ellen was here. It provided a sense of nostalgia, bringing Ellen back to their date here years ago. They were still young in their relationship when they came here the last time and Ellen smiled at the memory.

She followed Ryan to the barn as he gathered everything together to get the horses ready. "I'm surprised you even remember how to do all of this," Ellen teased him.

"Some things you just never forget, no matter where life takes you." He turned to look at her as he pulled his horse, Thor, from his stall. Ellen caught the meaning behind his words. No matter what had transpired between them all those years ago and no matter where life had taken them since that moment, they never forgot each other and here they were now. Together again.

Ellen helped Ryan saddle Thor and lead him to the tethering post outside. Majesty was neighing softly in her stall as Ryan grabbed the gear to get her ready to ride. Ellen was excited to see the horse was still here. Ellen stroked her velvety nose as Ryan got her saddled up. He led Majesty outside the barn to where Thor was located and helped Ellen mount her. It came back to her fairly easily and she got on the back of Majesty with no trouble. Majesty stood in place as she waited for Ryan to mount Thor and off they went down the trail.

Ellen was excited to see the view from the mountain again. Last time the trees didn't have leaves on them yet, but now that it was summer time, everything would be several, luscious shades of green.

They took their time navigating the trail, knowing they had all day to enjoy it. Ryan had a picnic lunch strapped to the side of Thor and they planned to stop halfway to eat it. Last night they had made their own special pasta salad to go with their ham sandwiches and a chocolate pie for dessert. Ellen's stomach was starting to grumble since she had forgotten to eat breakfast, so she was really looking forward to their picnic lunch.

They rode in silence, taking in the beauty around them. Ellen took the time to reflect on everything that had happened over the years. It was truly a miracle in some ways that they were even here together. Ryan's accident could have been deadly and she was so thankful that God had spared him, allowing her the opportunity to be with him now.

Ryan paused near a clearing in the woods, "This looks like the perfect spot to devour our lunch. Plus, I'm starving and I want to eat now."

Ellen giggled and dismounted her horse. They tied the horses to two trees near the clearing, allowing them to rest in the shade.

Ryan spread out the blanket they had packed and set the food out. He grabbed Ellen's hands and said a quick prayer of thanks for this day together.

They chatted about their week as they enjoyed the food. "I'm so glad we could come out here again," Ellen remarked.

Ryan swallowed a bite of his pie and nodded his agreement. He hadn't talked much today, which was unusual, but Ellen didn't think too much about it. He had a lot going on with trying to figure out his next step in life and Ellen figured he was just overwhelmed by that.

They finished their lunch and got back on their horses, continuing their journey to the top of the mountain. The anticipation of seeing the view again had Ellen's adrenaline pumping and she urged Majesty to move a little faster. Ryan nudged Thor to keep up with them and soon the clearing on the top of the mountain came into view.

Ellen inhaled deeply as she looked out over the amazing landscape. The sky was a vibrant shade of blue, dotted by a few fluffy clouds. Everything displaying the magnificence of God's handiwork. She tied Majesty to a tree and Ryan did the same with Thor. Ellen stepped towards the edge and took in a deep breath of the sweet, fresh air. Ryan came up behind her and slid his arms around her waist. He kissed the top of her head and the two of them stood in silence, taking in the beauty around them.

Ryan turned her around, so they could face each other; his eyes glistened with tears. "Ellie I brought you here today, because today is special. The last time I brought you here was a turning point for me. That day I realized that you were the one. You were the one I was going to spend forever with. The day I met you in the cafeteria I could sense something special about you. After all these years, it finally makes sense to me, the thought I had back then." He paused to clear his throat.

Ellen wasn't sure where this was going, but her heart was caught in her throat. She loved this man with her entire soul.

Ryan squeezed her hands and continued. "Our relationship grew that day; it grew into the beginning of a lifetime together. Sure, we've had some bumps along the way and some major life changes, but here we are now and we're together. We are blessed Ellie, beyond blessed and I feel honored that God has allowed me to be the man in your life. Now, if you'll allow me to be the man of your life for the rest of our time here on earth, I'll be able to mark this day as the most special one yet."

Her eyes burned with tears and a lump began to form in her throat, Ellen realized right then what Ryan was up to and her heart was bursting with joy.

Ryan let go of her left hand and reached into his pocket as he got down on one knee. "My dearest Ellie, will you be wife?" He pried open a small, black box to reveal shimmery diamonds, set in white gold.

Ryan's face blurred as the tears came. Ellen nodded her head up and down vigorously and let out a whispered yes between happy sobs.

Ryan jumped up and hugged her, lifting her from the ground and spinning her around. "Ellie, I am the happiest man alive right now." He set her down and slid the beautiful ring onto her finger. Ellen held her hand out letting the sunshine hit it, sending brilliant sparkles everywhere.

"I'm going to become Mrs. Ryan Salas," she shouted to the world. The horses perked up their ears and turned to look at them. It's almost as if they knew what was going on.

Ryan grabbed her face and kissed her, the salt from their happy tears mixing together, like the ocean waves kissing the sandy shore.

Ellen touched her nose to his and whispered so softly, not even the trees could hear, "You have made me the happiest woman alive. Thank you for loving me, Ryan."

Ryan kissed her lips and whispered back, "Baby, loving you is the easiest thing I've ever had to do."

They stood their kissing, drowning in the blissful moment. Their lives changing for the better, together. The sun began to set and the two of them curled up on the large flat rock to watch. The same rock they had sat on together all those years ago. Back then, neither of them would have known what God would do with their lives, but here they were now, engaged and ready to spend forever together.

Ryan had brought a lantern along with them, so they were able to see their way back down the mountain, but they didn't need it. The iridescent glow of the moon illuminated their path. It made the moment even more romantic. They made their way back to the barn, brushing down the horses and putting them back in their stalls.

Ellen walked out of the barn ahead of Ryan towards the Jeep, but when she looked, there were a few other cars parked in the gravel driveway. It wasn't light enough to see whose they were; a cloud was blocking the moonlight. "Are your Aunt and Uncle having company tonight?"

Ryan looked at the cars, "They must be. I still want to go in and thank them though for allowing us to come up here today."

Ellen hesitated, "Are you sure you want to bother them while they have company? I think that would be slightly rude."

"Nah, it'll be fine. Come on." Ryan reached for her hand.

Ellen took it and followed him up the lane to his Aunt and Uncle's spacious farmhouse. She really hoped they didn't mind them barging in on them.

Ryan gently knocked on the door and turned the knob.

"Ryan! You can't just walk in!" Ellen shrieked.

"I do it all the time."

Ellen wanted to scold him again, but was startled by a shout of "Surprise!" The room was filled with close family and friends, including Katie, who was beautifully tanned from her honeymoon.

"Oh my gosh!" She playfully punched Ryan on the arm. "You planned a surprise party?"

He winked and led her into the room where they both received many hugs and congratulations on their engagement.

Ellen's heart had never felt this full or wonderfully happy.

~*~

Three Months Later…

Even for November, the sun sent its warm rays down on them. Ellen was thankful for the unseasonably warm day. It was going to make their wedding day even more special. Katie finished Ellen's hair and makeup, just like Ellen had done for her. "My friend, you are stunning!" she exclaimed when she was finished. The girls embraced and tried their best to hold back the tears. Katie had told her earlier that morning that the moment she had seen Ellen with Ryan for the first time, she knew something special was going to happen in their lives and here she was witnessing it. "It's been like a 'Nicholas Sparks' movie for you two and I'm ecstatic to see that a happy ending is just around the corner."

Ellen was beaming. They had planned the wedding quickly, she and Ryan both ready to be together as husband and wife. They were having a small beach ceremony right outside her parents' cottage. The reception would be in their backyard. As Katie's wedding was, Ryan and Ellen chose to have a small gathering of close family and friends. The small, private beach behind her parents' home was perfect to avoid any potential media interrupting their special day.

Ellen adjusted her veil slightly and stood up from her chair. She stepped out onto the back deck and took her father's arm.

His eyes glistened as he took in the sight of her. "Beautiful, my darling. Just beautiful." He dabbed at the corner of his eye with a tissue he pulled from his jacket pocket. Ellen watched as her mother and future mother-in-law began the walk down towards the shore. Katie followed them in her turquoise gown, a small bouquet of white lilies in her hand.

Ellen took a deep breath, holding back the tears that threatened to fall. She fell in step with her dad as they made their way towards the aisle of sand.

When they rounded the corner, Ellen took in everything around her. The sandy beach, expansive ocean and most importantly her husband to be, smiling broadly at the sight of his bride. Ellen could see the tears slowly streaming down his cheeks the closer she got to him. Tears began to fight their way down her own cheeks as well, the intensity of the moment sinking in. This was it.

Her father kissed her cheek and handed her over to Ryan. She took his hands and let out a shaky breath. She had never been happier than she was in this moment, because after everything she had been through, God had blessed her with this, a second chance.

EPILOGUE

One Year Later...

Life was blissful, simply blissful. Their lives together as one truly had begun and continued as a fairytale. Sure, there were the usual marital bumps along the way over the past year, but Ryan wouldn't trade this for anything in the world.

His life felt complete now. He was coaching a local high school football team, a position he had felt called to be in. Ellen was writing again, this time for her own personal blog. She enjoyed it and wrote about all kinds of things going on in life. Her dream was to mentor young girls, allowing them to see the second chances in their own lives, even if things seemed dark. So far, with her blog, she was making an impact and Ryan couldn't be more proud of her.

They had recently adopted their golden lab, Harley and were continuing to try to have a baby. They knew that would come in God's time and Ryan was thankful that things in their life had been going so well.

He had a special evening planned for their one-year anniversary and he couldn't wait to surprise his Ellie. He hoped this would be the start of many, many more anniversaries together, because as he told her all the time… He was going to love her forever.

Made in the USA
Middletown, DE
04 July 2017